Her Sister's M
By Tabitha S

Cover Image Credits:
Design is a compilation by Tabitha Short
Photography by Tabitha Short
Tristee Brushes from Deviant Art
Amorphiss from Deviant Art
4shared Brushes
MiloArtDesign
Big Stock Photo

The First Five Pages Publications
Copyright 2012

ISBN-13:
978-1480292116
ISBN-10:
1480292117

License Notes

CHAPTER ONE

"Oh come on, it's not for real," her friend persuaded.

They had been walking toward the river to meet with their friends from school, but were early and decided to take a detour around the block. She stood looking toward the old house out of the corner of her eye. She'd seen it a million times before and knew the woman who lived there was a proclaimed psychic. She always wondered if anyone ever actually went inside, if the woman was ever able to actually make money. The sign that was near the sidewalk was quite old and hung from its hinges. As it swayed in the wind, she could imagine it making an eerie squeaking noise. It would be the perfect haunted house for any Halloween.

"I don't know, Abby. Forty dollars is a lot of money," she said. Forty dollars was a good chunk of the money she had saved from working at the Save-A-Lot over the summer.

"Fine," Abby said, rolling her eyes. "I'll pay. It'll be your birthday present!" Kate sometimes despised her friend's lack of frugality. Abby belonged to one of the richest families in the area, so she had never really had to contend with a budget. Kate definitely didn't want to spend forty whole dollars on something like a psychic reading, but she had no other excuse to throw at Abby. Kate huffed through her nose as she started up the walkway. Maybe the woman didn't actually do readings anymore. Maybe the old sign was a remnant of an old hobby. Or maybe no one was home.

The door was massive and looked like it weighed a ton. It was made of thick, heavy, dark wood and it arched inward up at the top, gothic-style. Around the trim were small symbols that looked as though they had been burned into the wood.

Abby knocked on the front door using the old door knocker. When they heard no one stirring on the other side, Abby knocked harder. They stood at the door momentarily before Abby grew frustrated and began knocking on the door incessantly with her fist.

She yelled into the wind, "Hello? Hello?"

Kate ran her finger across the strange symbols along the door. She wondered what they meant. Then she noticed a sign peeking through thin vines growing up the side of the house. She pushed the vines away and another sign that was a miniature replica of the one in the yard read, 'Please come to the side door.'

"Stop," Kate said to Abby, placing her arm between Abby's knuckles and the door. Abby's yelling and knocking ceased. Kate pointed at the sign and Abby's eyes squinted to try to read it.

"Look," Kate said with her arm and finger extended.

"Oh," Abby said acknowledging the sign.

They made their way around to the side of the house. A large wooden fence separated them from the backyard and the side door. Kate expected it to be rusted shut, but to her surprise, it opened easily and without a sound.

Although Kate found it strange that such an old fixture wouldn't squeak when opened, Abby took no notice of it and hurried through the gate, pulling Kate behind her. Abby giggled with excitement as they made their way through the tall, dying grass to the door.

Abby raised her fist to the door, but before she could lay her knuckles to the old wood, the door creaked open. *Just like in a creepy movie,* Kate thought.

"Oh you got to be kidding me, really?" Abby said with a guffaw and a chuckle.

They walked through the door and a light, fog-like mist flooded the floor. A strobe light somewhere in the back kicked on and eerie noises and witch cackles filled the air. They were poorly done effects. Kate rolled her eyes. But then she felt something at her feet. It was warm and Kate's heart beat fast as she felt it slither between her legs. Her breath caught in her throat and her heart lurched. It entangled in her feet, and she felt a scream rise up in her throat as she began imagining what kind of animal it could be. When a snake crossed her mind she could not contain her scream any longer.

"Ahh!" She erupted, turning and running out of the house.

"What? What happened?" Abby yelled to her, running after her. Kate was fumbling with the latch on the gate, trying desperately to get it open.

From behind them, they heard a human laugh; a low, sultry chuckle.

Kate turned and there stood a large, dark-skinned Native American woman with her arms crossed. Half her face had no smile or emotion while the other half laughed dramatically. Her large belly bounced up and down with each huff of breath.

"I didn't sink zat ould work so well," the woman said out of the corner of her mouth. Kate realized the left side of the woman's face was paralyzed.

"Please, come in." Her words were slow, pressed and deliberate.

"It was only a zoke," she said, stumbling over her last word.

Kate saw Abby's body relax and watched her face turn into a smile. Kate only relaxed when she saw a large black cat scurry out of the open side door and wrap itself around the large legs of the woman. It must have been what had snaked around her legs: just a fury cat.

"You are here for a reading?" The woman asked slowly, careful with the sounds of the words.

"We are," Abby said, lacing her arm through Kate's arm.

"Well, come in zin," she said, turning and picking up the black cat. The cat let out a small meow as he was lifted to nuzzle in the crook of the woman's large neck.

The two girls followed the old, wrinkly woman through the door. This time, there was no fog, no strobe lighting or any eerie sounds that, in retrospect, Kate could identify were obviously from the c.d. player in the corner. They made their way across the room, which Kate could identify as being a garage as it had concrete floors and an unfinished ceiling. Up some stairs and through another door and they were in the old woman's kitchen.

"Please, excuse ze mess," she said, but there was no mess. Everything was clean and neat. The kitchen smelled of lemon and the floor shined as if it had just been mopped. There were no dishes in the sink. The table was set, complete with the nicest plate set and prettiest cloth napkins Kate had ever seen. In the corner sat a large buffet with a hutch, which displayed an extensive tea cup collection. The countertops were marble, or resembled marble, and the appliances were stainless steel. It was modern inside, which did not match the antique-like outside.

There was a small entryway at the opposite end of the kitchen. Kate guessed it was from the entrance of the front door. Just past it was an entrance into a room. Kate could see a large bay window and recliner chair near it. The rest of the room wrapped around the corner and was unseen. To the right of the entrance was a door, one that Kate assumed led to a closet, but the woman walked right to it and opened it wide. It was dark inside and Kate had second thoughts until the woman pulled on a small cord and the light flicked on. It was much larger inside than Kate had expected. It was a circular room that didn't appear to have walls. Instead there were thick carpet-like tapestries that hung from ceiling to floor. Perhaps the room wasn't circular at all, but the tapestries confined the open space to the shape.

Kate watched as the woman took a seat at the small table opposite the door.

"Please, zit down," she said.

The two girls sat down in the chairs in front of them.

"Who is hirst?" The woman asked slowly.

"Ooooh, she is," Abby said, pointing at Kate excitedly.

"And your payment?" The woman asked.

"Oh, that's me," Abby said, stuffing her hand into her pocket and pulling out a wad of twenties.

The woman held her hand out and accepted the bills as if they were contaminated. She dumped them in a small dish on a small round table beside her.

"Alright," the woman said, wiggling herself into her chair to get comfortable. She closed her eyes, breathed in through her nose and breathed out through the roundness of the right side of her mouth. She held her hands out and tilted her head upward. One more deep breath in and out and slowly her eyes opened as she brought her gaze up to meet Kate's eyes.

She held her hands out, suggesting Kate place her hands in her grasp. Kate quickly put her hands into the woman's, who flinched at the notion of someone else touching her.

"You must make sree wishes. Zen tell me only one of zee wishes," she instructed.

Kate thought for a moment. She thought about her grades, they were never so hot. She thought about her mother who cried a lot because she was a single parent and money was always so difficult. Kate thought about the boy she had a crush on, Adam. Adam was also, unfortunately, the boy Abby had a crush on. But Abby didn't know her secret. Finally Kate made her wishes in her mind.

I wish for my mother to be happy. I wish Adam would choose me to be his girlfriend. I wish I had better grades. There. Those were her wishes. Before she chose one to tell to the psychic, she paused to make sure they were the wishes she wanted to use. They sounded so petty when she thought about them, but they were honestly what she wanted most. Or were they? Kate grappled with herself to change one or two of them to something that mattered, like better treatment of women in Muslim countries, or food for the hungry.

"Now, tell me one of your wishes," the woman said, breaking up Kate's self-argument.

Kate cleared her throat and chose the one wish she didn't mind Abby hearing.

"I wish for my mother to be happy," she said. *At least ONE of my wishes isn't selfish*, she thought to herself.

The woman concentrated on the hands she held in her own. She gripped them tight, but not tight enough to cause Kate to be uncomfortable. She closed her eyes and took several deep breaths in and out. Finally, with one last squeeze, the woman released Kate's hands and quickly brought her arms to rest in her lap. Slowly she opened her eyes. Kate wondered if all of the dramatics was just for show, like the setup in the garage.

"It appears as though your life began before you were born," the woman said. *Seriously? Yeah, this is a joke*, she thought. Kate was disappointed. How can someone's life begin before they are born and how vague is something like that? She couldn't believe she let Abby talk her into doing this.

"There was someone before you, someone called Loraine; a seester. Did your mother have a daughter before you?" She asked.

A stone flopped in Kate's stomach and her breath was taken away. Kate did have a sister. But her sister disappeared two years before Kate was even born.

Thoughts flooded Kate's mind. She remembered her mother telling her how she had disappeared one afternoon from their cousin's front porch. She remembered her mother telling her they couldn't find any suspects and never found a body. Her sister, Loraine, vanished without a trace. Her stomach convulsed inside of its hold, lurching and squirming. It felt like it was making the motions of vomiting, but there was no vomit in her throat. She wanted to tell the woman to stop, but she was so shocked to hear it out of someone's mouth that she was speechless. Her sister had vanished in a town a thousand miles away. No one knew of her mother's past in the small West Virginian town in which they'd been living.

"Zee was kidnapped, yes?" The woman asked.

"Yes," Kate heard herself say.

"It has dictated your mother's life. It is why zeee cries so hard at night," the woman said. Kate could not draw her voice again. Had she subconsciously always blamed it on money problems?

"I see an inevitable trouble in a close relazionzip. You will lose zomezing, but gain zomezing else," the woman said. "The zing lost will be forever, you will not have it again."

Kate tore herself away from the torturing memories of her mother's pain and began thinking about what she had that she might lose and quickly became frustrated with the vagueness. She hoped the woman was not talking about her mother. She could never stand losing her mother.

"You will zet out on a zourney soon," the woman continued. She opened the side of her mouth to say more, but then her brows creased in confusion. She sat that way for what seemed like a long time.

"It is hazy. Zometimes the future is like zat; zometimes it depends on the person's decisions. You have a decision to make, a big one," she finished.

"Can you be a little clearer?" Abby chimed in, a hint of sarcasm in her voice.

The woman looked up at Kate and the unparalyzed part of her face began to contort into what Kate believed to be deep sorrow.

"You have a connection to your zeester that you are unaware of at zee moment," she said rather fast for her condition.

"zhe will help you find what you need. Zat is all," she concluded and then turned to Abby. Kate's heart sank, she needed to know more than that.

Abby jiggled her feet in anticipation as she slapped her hands down into the psychic's hands. The woman flinched at the touch again.

"I already have my wishes. I wish for Adam to ask me to the Enchantment and Charms Prom," she said quickly, her knees bouncing up and down with excitement.

The woman rubbed her fingers over Abby's knuckles. Her display of 'honing' in on a person was not as elaborate as the one she did for Kate.

"You too will lose zomezing. You will hurt greatly for a while, but will soon be disracted by zange of scenery. Your life will take a big shift. Not now, but in a while. You will move overzeez. Your education is big in your life and you will have many adventures and fun times. You love to cook and to bake, don't you? I see meat pies, gourmet dinner, elaborate cakes..." the woman trailed off.

"Oh yes, I love to cook!" Abby interrupted. "Will I be a chef or a baker?" She asked.

"You will do zomezing around food and it will take you many different places," she finished. The lady breathed in deep and released her hands from Abby.

"Aww, can't you tell me more? What about Adam? Will I get married? Will I go to Italy?" Abby asked.

The woman smiled a big smile and said simply, "your life is a happy one while you are young. It will be whatever zoo want it to be and whatever zoo make it."

Abby's reading had not distracted Kate at all and she was ready to leave. She hated being reminded of the source of her mother's pain. She hated the feeling that seemed to stick with her for hours after thinking about her missing sister. She hated it so much that she never let herself think about what her sister might have been like. Every time those thoughts crept into her mind she would distract herself because she knew inevitably it would lead her to the pain of her mother and she could not bear it.

Back on the sidewalk Abby said gently, "you never told me you had a sister."

"I never knew her. She disappeared before I was born," was all Kate could manage to say.

Something stuck in Kate's throat and she couldn't yet voice all the things her mother had told her about the situation and she couldn't share them with Abby.

Abby was silent for the first time all day. All her previous giddiness had faded. Kate had always appreciated Abby's ability to know when things bothered people. She could tell Abby wanted to ask more questions so Kate took a deep breath and fought against the music inside of her that asked her not to continue. She explained as best she could.

"She had gone to see our cousin who lived a block away, but when she got there our cousin was babysitting her younger siblings and couldn't hang out with her. That was the last time she was seen. Our cousin said she went out the door and she assumed she had gone home. A neighbor across the street reported looking out her window and seeing my sister sitting on my cousin's porch." It was all Kate knew. It was all anyone knew.

Abby was quiet, as if she were taking in the information. She walked with her hands in her pockets, staring down at her shoes as she walked. Kate assumed she was concentrating on figuring out the right way to probe further into Abby's mother's past. But Abby was silent the rest of the way.

For the rest of the evening Kate was distracted by thoughts of the sister she never knew. She had never allowed herself to think on it so much, but the words of the psychic kept gnawing at her. How did the psychic know of her sister? She would have known by all the newspaper and media coverage it had attracted, but that was a long time ago and a thousand miles away. How could she possibly know that story was linked to Kate?

She must just keep information on everyone in town, so that when they come to visit her she can pretend to tell them their past so they'll believe her when she tells them their 'future,' she thought.

Kate knew that was just as impossible as having real psychic powers. How can one person know everything about everyone in town? And what about the tourists who stop by? The quiet, sleepy town had a booming tourism industry due to its architectural beauty and ancient cemeteries. There were many bed and breakfasts, hotels and historical sites that were said to be haunted. How could she know about the lives of those people? Did she even get many people into her home for readings?

The thoughts followed her home that night after hanging out with her friends and she found herself lying awake in bed, unable to sleep because of it. Her mother was still at work, she wouldn't be home until 11:00 p.m. Kate was usually asleep by then. She decided that if she were still awake when her mother got home, she would try to bring herself to ask her mother about the lost sister. She had only asked on two other occasions and both times she listened to her mother cry herself to sleep through the walls. She didn't want to remind her mother again of the child she had lost.

But Kate drifted slowly to sleep, dreaming of walking along the lake with Abby and their friends. She dreamt they were playing hide-go-seek in the great cemetery downtown just after dark. She and Abby crouched down behind a large trash bin and covered their mouths to try to stifle their giggles.

"Oh I got to pee so badly," Kate whispered to her friend.

"Hold it till this round is over," Abby smiled back.

Kate had no other choice and she peeked around the can to see if the seeker was anywhere near them. She could see no one. The cemetery turned completely silent and, for the first time that night, scary. She felt alone. Turning back to her friend, she discovered Abby was gone. Abby's laugh echoed in the night.

"Abby," she whispered, hoping Abby had only skipped over to hide behind a tombstone. The small laugh grew faint.

When she received no response she whispered louder, "Abby?" The laughing had stopped.

Kate was about to whisper again, this time a little louder when she felt someone come up on her from behind.

"You won't find her," she heard a male voice say.

"What do you mean?" Kate asked. She had a feeling of impending doom. Somehow she knew what he had already told her. She knew she wouldn't be seeing Abby again.

"You won't find her. She isn't here. She is gone," he said in a frightened voice. Abby realized the boy seemed developmentally delayed.

"Where is she?" Kate asked, standing up. Her body flooded with anger and she did not know why. It was just a silly game, but for some reason she felt like it was so much more.

The boy stood still with a sad look on his face. He was big and bulky and looked like he felt guilty, like he was distraught. Something in his face made Kate understand that Abby was not just gone, she was dead. The despair flooded through her body, washing away the anger. Pain settled in her chest and a lump in her throat appeared and she heard the horrible pain-induced sounds coming from deep within her. She fell to her knees as the sharp, heart-breaking pain seared through her heart.

Kate woke up whimpering. The pain she felt in the dream clung to her, like the stench of cigarette smoke clung to her Uncle Mark. Even as she got out of bed, her heart still ached for a best friend that never really died.

The dream had felt so real. Kate lay back down in bed trying to shake the feeling and go back to sleep. Eventually her heartbeat slowed and the warmth returned to her eyelids as they fluttered closed and she drifted away.

CHAPTER TWO

All during school the next day Kate was distracted by thoughts of how to ask her mother about the sister she never knew; about Loraine. She needed help, she wanted advice but she didn't want to share the personal story with Abby. They were unhappy things; bad things and she didn't want it to be a part of her Abby world. Her Abby world was full of fun and happiness. This was something different, something she felt she needed to keep hidden in order to spare herself and her mother the questions that people ask and the attention they get from it.

In computer class she was sitting at her computer and she remembered quite vividly the microphones and flashing cameras that were pushed in her face when they had tried to go out. It had happened when Kate was four. The police had said they had found a new lead. A man had been arrested and convicted of kidnapping and murdering another little girl and they thought he might have kidnapped Loraine six years before. Kate remembered feeling scared when they would try to go out. Looking back on it, she imagined her mother must have been a ball of emotions. It was never confirmed that the man was the abductor. She remembered her mother crying a lot that year and having to stay with her grandmother. She wouldn't do it. She would not ask her mother to think about Loraine. Not again.

An instant message from Cora popped up on her screen. She looked across the room at Cora, who smiled. Before Kate could read the message she got an idea. Google it. Or Bing it, whichever would get the most results the fastest. Obviously it had been saturated in the media, not once, but twice in the past. There would be articles to read.

And then Kate thought about the microfilm machine at the library. The library would have slides from newspapers in their archives. Would they have slides from the newspaper where they had lived at the time her sister disappeared? There probably would not be any there in Change Modei. Change Modei was a small town in the central part of West Virginia. She'd have to take a plane to Charlotte, North Carolina to find the archives she needed! *Okay, maybe that's an exaggeration,* she thought. So first, the internet.

Kate's mouth was dry and she licked her lips as she put the soft underside of her fingers to the keys. Slowly she typed, "Loraine Margaret Cooper Charlotte North Carolina." Her screen was flooded with links to missing persons websites. She clicked on missingkids.com and found the National Center for Missing and Exploited Children. Three profiles of children who had recently gone missing in the US were posted front and center on the homepage. Underneath was a box to put in information to refine a search of the website. Kate checked the box for 'female' and scrolled down to find 'North Carolina' in the drop down box provided. In the 'Missing within ___ years' prompt, Kate plugged in nineteen.

Kate was shocked with what she found. Staring back at her from her computer screen was the fourteen year old face of the sister she never knew. Kate recognized her immediately from the few pictures her mother had shown her. In fact, she remembered seeing this very same picture. Loraine's profile was the only profile listed for that date range. Kate clicked on it.

Before the page could load, the bell rang to switch classes. Her next class was on another floor and on the other side of the building. She barely had time to stop at her locker between her computer class and her English class. But today she didn't care about being late to class. What she needed was to read Loraine's profile.

Beside the picture of her sister was more information.
DOB: March 3, 1979
Missing: June 15, 1993
Age Now: 32
Sex: F
Race: White Caucasian
Hair: Brown
Eyes: Brown
Height: 5'2"
Weight: 125
Missing from: Charlotte, North Carolina

Loraine Margaret Cooper, last seen at a relative's house on the front porch in Charlotte, North Carolina. Loraine is believed to have been abducted.

ANYONE HAVING INFORMATION SHOULD CONTACT
National Center for Missing & Exploited Children
1-800-843-5678 (1-800-THE-LOST)
Missing Children Division 699 Prince Street, Alexandria, VA 22314

It was information she already knew Kate clicked the back button and went through two or three more profiles before she heard the tardy bell ring. Kids for the next computer class were coming into the classroom so she began to click as many links as she could and quickly read everything.

Before long she heard the long, drawn out sigh and the smacking of gum. Kate was at the computer the girl was assigned and she was obviously impatient. Kate recognized the girl from the dance team and rolled her eyes at the girl's snottiness. She stood with one hand on her hip, blowing bubbles with her gum, picking at her fingernails and sighing every chance she got in an attempt to hurry Kate out of the way.

When the bell rang for class to start, Kate gave up. She decided she would come back after school to see what else she could find. She grabbed her bag and raced out the door and up the stairs.

***

"There you are, holy cow, where were you?" Abby asked, leaning up against the hood of her convertible. The school parking lot was almost deserted.

"I was getting ready to leave you, you know," she added as Kate scuttled to the passenger side.

"Sorry, I totally forgot," Kate said. She had told Abby they would go shopping for dresses after school. Somehow, shopping for dresses didn't seem as important as it had a few days ago. But she had found nothing new on the search engines after her last class.

In the car, Kate had the feeling Abby knew everything. It felt odd keeping something so big away from her closest friend. Abby was her only friend really. Then she remembered Cora's instant message. She hadn't even responded to it.

"Shit," Kate said and fished her cell phone out from her purse. She texted Cora as fast as her fingers would go and apologized for not responding and asked her what she had messaged her earlier.

"Who are you texting?" Abby asked.

"Cora, she messaged me in computer class, but I totally ignored it," Kate said.

Abby grumbled and said, "I am so mad at her."

"Why?" Kate asked.

"She asked Adam to the prom and she *knows* I'm waiting for him to ask me. I've been dropping hints to him all week. Everyone knows I want to go with him," she said.

"She just wants your attention," Kate said, trying to reassure her friend.

"Nobody even started liking him until I did," Abby complained. But Kate knew that wasn't true at all. Abby forgot most things that didn't have much to do with Abby and she must have forgotten that Kate had told her she thought he was cute a long time ago. They had been in middle school at the time and had only just met. That was five years ago.

"He'll choose you, Abs," Kate said, punching in a response to Cora's text.

Cora had been trying to tell Kate something. Her text back read, "I need to tell you a secret. It's something you'll *really* want to hear. Call me. But not when you're with Abby."

Kate imagined it had something to do with Adam. She imagined Cora was going to the prom with him and wanted to tell Kate all about it, but didn't want Abby to know. But Kate didn't understand why, Abby would find out soon enough. Kate drew in a breath. *Oh the drama,* she thought as she considered dropping her own crush for the boy just because too many other girls wanted to be his girlfriend.

Kate had responded simply, "OK."

"What is she saying?" Abby asked.

"She wants to study for our computer class test coming up," Kate lied. She was amazed at how easy it came to her.

"How can you study for a computer class?" Abby asked.

Kate laughed out loud. There was a textbook that came with the class, one that no one read. But every so often there were tests on the information from the book. But for some reason the curriculum chosen for their grade level was well beneath what all the students already knew. No one ever studied for computer class; it was far too easy.

"I don't know," Kate answered.

"She's trying to steal you from me, why is she so obsessed with us?" Abby said.

"No she's not. And you don't have to worry, I'll be finding out if she asked Adam to the prom because she likes him or if she did it just to get under your skin," Kate said.

After that Abby must have felt reassured enough to drop the subject.

At the mall Abby was in a dressing room, trying on a short pink mini dress when Kate's phone vibrated. Looking down at it she saw the text was from Cora.

'I REALLY need 2 tell u something very important. R U home yet?' The text read.

'No,' Kate typed back. 'I'm shopping with Abby.'

Her phone sat still in her pocket for the next ten minutes. She felt it vibrate as Abby was mid-sentence trying to convince Kate to try on a dress that had a neckline much lower than Kate was comfortable with.

"I have to use the restroom, keep looking for one with a purple bustier," Kate said.

Kate walked out of the store and into the mall. She looked back to make sure Abby was distracted looking for a dress. Instead of going into the restroom, Kate sneaked around the corner and went out the exit.

The cool air blew her hair up and out as she quickened her pace to get around the corner. She felt safe enough to make the phone call. It rang three times before Cora answered.

"Hey," she said. "Are you still with Abby?"

"I'm outside," Kate answered, "hurry up and tell me, it's freezing."

"Well," Cora started. "This morning I was talking to Adam. I was trying to find out if he was going to ask Abby to the prom. I mean, she blatantly wants to go with him. So I was talking to him and asked him straight out who he wanted to go with. He wouldn't answer me, just got all blushy the way he does. So I started naming off some girls and he would shake his head no. So then I named

Abby and thought for sure he'd turn away or something or not answer me or whatever, but he didn't. So then I was kind of mad--"

"He doesn't want to go with Abby?" Kate asked, interrupting her. She was stunned. Everyone wanted to go to the prom with Abby. Abby was the freaking 'it' girl. She was thin, had money, a convertible and long blonde hair and blue eyes. Who in their right mind *wouldn't* want to take Abby to the prom?

"No, Kate. He wants to go with you," she said. Kate's heart stopped. Surely it was a mistake. She didn't think he even knew she existed. Cora had to be mistaken.

"Kate?" Cora breathed into the phone.

"Are...are you sure?" Kate asked.

"Yes. After I asked about Abby he said, 'close' so then I named Rami and he said 'back to cold' and then it hit me. YOU. So I asked him and he just smiled. He told me not to tell anyone, but I thought you'd want to know," she said.

"Um, yeah. Thanks Cora," Kate said. She was stunned and absentmindedly flipped her phone shut. As it closed she could hear Cora asking, "What are you going to do?"

What *would* she do? Part of her was overjoyed and shocked that Adam not only knew who she was, but wanted to take her to a prom. Part of her was worried about what would happen with Abby if she agreed to go with him. Part of her was angry at herself for even considering it when she knew her friend liked him so much. What *was* she going to do?

Kate went back into the mall to find Abby. Abby was paying for a dress at the counter. It was the pink mini dress. Kate thought she would need a cardigan to go over it, but she knew Abby wouldn't get one. Kate still did not have a dress. She wondered if she'd even go to the prom now. Her stomach squirmed.

"So the mini, then?" Kate asked, happy to pretend nothing was happening.

"Yeah, it's cute right?" Abby said, holding it up to her. Kate couldn't really make out much through the plastic that covered it.

"I think it's perfect," she said. And she meant it. It was a really nice dress and fit Abby perfectly.

"Now for you," Abby said.

"Maybe on another day. I'm not feeling so well," Kate said. And she didn't, for many reasons.

"Oh no, you're not getting sick, are you?" Abby asked.

"It might have been something I ate, my stomach isn't so good," Kate said.

Abby made a face that seemed to say 'gross,' so Kate suggested they go home. On the way it was oddly quiet in the car. Obviously Abby was distracted and Kate wondered what she was thinking about. She couldn't knock the feeling that Abby knew all about her hunt for information about Loraine and now she felt Abby somehow knew all about Adam.

When they pulled into the drive way of Kate's house, Abby shut the engine off. Kate could see the furrow on her brow.

"Why do you think some people are that way?" Abby asked. Kate's heart stopped thinking it confirmed she knew about Adam.

"What way?" Kate asked, hoping she was wrong.

"Like Cora. One minute she's all about being our friend and wanting to hang out with us and then the next she's...you know...backstabbing us. Or me, I guess. Why do people have to be that way?" Abby asked, solemnly.

Kate's heart hurt. She felt like she was the one who was backstabbing. But was it really? She didn't know.

"I don't know," was all she could muster for a response.

"Well, I'm really glad we're friends, Kate. I don't know how I would view people if I didn't have you," she said. Then she smiled real big and added, "you anchor my belief in people."

Once Abby smiled, Kate followed suit. She loved Abby's smile. She loved hearing her laugh and she loved how much fun they had together. She told herself she would not go to the prom with Adam if he asked her. She would concentrate on finding out information about her sister instead of thinking on the matter.

Kate walked in the door and slid her purse and backpack off her shoulder. They fell to the floor with a clunk. Kate looked through the mail on the small table to see if anything had come for her. There was nothing and so she went to her bedroom to try to search the internet once more for information on her sister.

She still couldn't find anything more than what she already knew. So she began searching for the name of the paper from Charlotte. She found it was called The Charlotte Observer. She found a way to search the archives and typed in her sister's name, but to her dismay the only articles that showed up were some kind of lists of scoreboard, which didn't make sense. She tried to refine the search by putting in the exact year she was looking for and discovered the online archives only went back to 1997, four years *after* her sister went missing.

Kate decided to try to call The Charlotte Observer to see how she could get access to the 1997 archives. The phone number was in the Contact Us section of the website.

When Kate retrieved her phone from her purse she saw she had a new text from Cora. It read, "Why does Abby think I asked Adam to the prom? Please tell her that I didn't, she won't answer my phone calls or texts."

Kate really didn't want to think about the predicament, so she ignored it. Instead she quickly punched in the number to the Charlotte newspaper. It rang four times before someone picked up the phone on the other end.

"Welcome to the Charlotte Observer, please listen carefully as our menu options have changed," the pre-recorded voice said. The voice went through all the options before she heard the one she was looking for at the end.

"For all other questions, press zero or stay on the line," the voice said.

Annoyed, Kate pressed zero.

"Charlotte Observer, how may I help you?" The non-automated male voice said.

"Hi, I'm trying to search through the archives online, but it only goes back to 1997. Do you have physical archives, like on microfilm or whatever, that goes back further?" She asked.

"Uh…" the man said, thinking. "I'm pretty sure you'd be able to find older archives at the library downtown. Would you like the address and phone number?"

"Yes, please," Kate said, readying a pencil over the pad of paper beside her desktop computer.

She scribbled down the information and then hung up and dialed the library. The voice on the other end had a slight southern drawl.

"Mecklenburg Library, may I help you?"

"Hi, I'm wondering if you keep archives of the Charlotte Observer and if they go back to 1993?"

"We do keep archives of the Observer and I believe they go back to 1985. Is there a specific article you're looking for? Perhaps I can bring it up and get it for you."

"Well, I'm not sure if any articles exist. I'm looking for any article on the disappearance of Loraine Margaret Cooper from 1993," Kate said.

"Let me have a look," the woman said slowly.

"You know, I remember when that happened. The little girl that went missing from her front porch," the lady said. At least she had some of the information correct. Kate didn't bother to correct her.

"Here we go, it looks like there are a few articles," the lady said.

"Is there a way I can access those online or have them faxed?" Kate asked.

"You can get them on our website, but you need to have a library card."

Kate sighed.

"Oh, I don't live in Charlotte," she said.

"Do you have any family or friends who live in Charlotte that have a library card?" The lady asked.

Kate did have family there. She remembered a grandmother living there. She remembered her grandmother as being very old and frail. She was very mean and never wanted Kate or her mother around. She had always insisted her son was not Kate's father. Kate would have been happy to agree, she didn't like her father much. He never wanted anything to do with her so why should she want anything to do with him? The last time she had seen him was when she was six. He and her mother had just split up and he showed up on his motorcycle just after midnight and started throwing bricks and mud at the house. One brick broke her bedroom window and she remembered being so scared she screamed and cried for hours while her mother called the police. The next morning they discovered he had destroyed their flower beds in the front yard and had strewn the plants across the yard. Kate had worked hard on their garden, learning the different plants and how to take care of them. She was very upset that her father would destroy them the way he did. It wasn't long after that when they packed up and moved to West

Virginia. Her Uncle Mark had a house he rented to them for cheap until her mother was able to find a job.

"Yes," she answered, just to end the conversation. "I'll contact them and see if they can get the information I need." Kate knew that was a lie. She would never contact her father *or* her grandmother.

"OK, good," the woman replied. "Just have them come down with you and if you call ahead I can have the microfilm all set up for you when you get here."

"OK," Kate said, knowing she would never be able to go to that library.

Frustrated, Kate lay on her bed. How was she going to get more information? She felt she had no other choice but to go to Charlotte. Perhaps she would be able to find more than old newspaper articles.

The sound of her phone vibrating on the desk startled her. Picking it up, she saw a text from Abby. It said, "I'm bored."

Kate wished she had Abby's help. She wished she had anybody's help. As Kate lay on her bed she remembered a few old boxes in the attic that had pictures and documents in them. She scurried off the bed and into the hallway to pull down the access stairs to the attic. Perhaps there was some fragment of information that would be useful.

Kate hated the attic. It was cold and dark and smelled like moth balls. Not only that, but there were spider webs everywhere. Kate hated spiders. As soon as the stairs retracted and hit the floor, a wave of fear swept over her. Attics were scary, especially this one.

Kate considered waiting until her mother got home to go up the stairs, but she was afraid her mother would ask her why she was up there and she couldn't think of a single excuse that would suffice.

She gripped the shaky side rails and slowly went up the stairs. When she got to the top she peeked over the boards. She could see her breath as she breathed out. Looking around, Kate made sure there were no wild animal eyes peering at her in the dark. Dust filled her nose and she sneezed as she lifted herself up onto the knotty pine boards.

The boxes were over in the corner near the window. She took a deep breath, stood up and walked to them slowly, the boards creaking under her weight. Through the window the sun was going down over the town. She opened the box on top and began going through all the papers and pictures that were inside. All the pictures were of her and her mother on some of the vacation trips they had taken in the past few years. She recognized all of them. They were all photos she had on her computer.

In the bottom of the box was the nightgown she adored when she was very young. She held it up and remembered how the soft cotton felt against her legs and how the ruffled top always itched. Holding it up, something caught her eye just beyond the nightgown, something out the window. Letting the gown fall back into the box she scooted closer to the window to see clearer.

CHAPTER THREE

It was Adam. He was hanging out on the corner of the street a block over. It looked like he was on his cell phone. Kate's heart skipped a beat the way it always did when she saw Adam. She thought of Abby and knew what she had to do. She left the documents and photos scattered on the dusty attic floor, scurried down the stairs and went out the front door.

Once outside, Kate slowed her step to try to slow her breathing. But she knew it wouldn't work, her heart raced in anticipation of actually talking to Adam. She could see his profile in the distance. The sun had slid its way almost completely over the horizon, leaving the streets in twilight.

His back was turned to her; she could see he was definitely on the phone. He wore a thin, black leather dress jacket. The collar was popped up and his dark hair was cut short with small spikes on the top. She was glad he didn't fall into the new fad of skinny jeans and punk shirts. She liked his khaki straight pants and clean cut features.

She was coming up on him. He must have heard her footsteps when she was about eight feet from him because he turned to face her. She thought she could see his eyes get big in the dark from the startle of seeing her.

"Uh, hi," Adam said, clicking his phone to hang it up. She was still walking toward him.

"Hi," she said with a squeaky voice. Perfect.

There was a moment of awkward silence then Kate blurted out, "I can't go to the prom with you." Her words stumbled over the next and it sounded like a mumble.

"I'm sorry?" Adam asked.

Kate took a breath and tried to speak slower. She hated what she was saying. "I can't go to the prom with you, I'm sorry."

Adam's shoulders shrank. The end of his mouth curled up and he smiled and said, "but I haven't even asked you yet."

Kate looked at her feet. For a moment she thought Cora must have been wrong, but he had said, 'yet.' So he was definitely planning to ask her at some point.

"I know," she said, looking down at her feet. "I don't want to go with you because I think you should ask Abby."

"Oh," was all he said. They both stood, looking down at their feet.

"I'm going to see my brother in a few weeks," Adam blurted. She could see him begin to sweat in spite of the cold February air. Obviously he was nervous. What a random subject to bring up. Kate blushed, embarrassed because she knew he was nervous.

"Oh?" She said, zipping her jacket and nestling her neck into it. She could see her breath.

She knew Adam felt awkward. She did, too. She didn't know what to say, she just knew she wanted their conversation to continue.

"Where is he?" She asked.

"He's at college. I'm going down to see him and check out the campus," he explained. Adam's brother Arthur was a year older than them. He was already in college; a freshman.

"Oh I meant, where does he go?" She clarified.

"Oh," Adam said, "he goes to Queens University"

"You're brave to drive in New York traffic!" Kate said, smiling.

"Not Queens, New York," Adam said. "Queens University in North Carolina"

Kate's breath caught in her chest. Did he just say North Carolina? Was this was her ticket to North Carolina? But how could she ask to go along? That would be really weird. It felt too easy.

"When did you say you were going?" Kate asked.

"In two weeks," he answered.

Good, this would give Kate enough time to figure out how to get invited along. Was this really happening? Did he really just say he was going to NC? Where in NC was Queens University? She'd have to look it up when she got home. Hopefully it was near Charlotte. Or perhaps Adam would have to travel past Charlotte to get to Queens University. She wanted to ask him, but as she glimpsed his side profile her heart sped up and she became instantly shy.

Adam was not the typical popular guy. He was not a jock. He was not a bad boy. He was not even one of those really cute nerd types. He was just average. He was not the quarterback; in fact he didn't even play football. He played baseball, but sat on the bench most of the time. He wasn't president of any clubs or organizations and didn't run for student council. He wore clothes that were plain, sometimes preppy, and sat with a group of other averages at lunch. His best friend was a boy named Carl who was homeschooled. Yet he somehow had the eye of nearly every girl in school. He was cute in the way that Johnny Depp was cute. His jaws were strong, his lips were perfect and his skin was neither dark nor light nor caramel colored. But the best feature was his eyes. Adam had dark eyes that were noticeable right away. They were warm and friendly. Kate couldn't count how many times she had dreamt of his eyes.

And now here she stood beside him, having an actual conversation.

"So," Kate said. "Do you think you'll ask Abby to prom?"

"Do you want me to?" He asked.

"Well, I mean, she really wants to go with you. No one else really, just you," she told him.

"If I do, will you save me a dance?" He asked.

Kate nuzzled her face into her collar to hide her big smile. Adam rubbed his hands together to create warmth. His hands were big, but not too big. They looked strong, yet soft. She wondered what it'd be like to feel their warmth wrapped around her or pulling her into him.

"We'll see," she said.

Adam smiled at her; he knew she was teasing and he liked it. Kate was a mystery to him, a quiet mystery. He knew nothing about her except that she lived with her mother and was Abby's friend. He had been on his way to ask her to the prom. He got halfway to her house when his phone rang. It had been Abby. She had called to chat like she had been doing for the past three days. She had been calling him around 7:00 p.m. every night. Adam didn't mind Abby at all. Abby was hot and fun. She was always smiling and happy and was very easy to talk to, but it was Kate that Adam wanted.

When Adam had turned to see Kate only a few feet from him, he had quickly said to Abby, "gotta go" and hung up abruptly. He hoped she wouldn't be angry at him for it later.

And now, before he even got the chance to ask Kate to the prom, Kate was telling him she wanted him to ask Abby. It was confusing to him, but he would do whatever to make Kate happy. Besides, Abby wasn't exactly undatable.

"Alright, I'll ask her," he said.

"Thanks," Kate said and turned to walk away. She was walking very slowly and got about ten feet from Adam when she heard footsteps right behind her.

As the steps got louder she turned to see Adam was catching up to her.

"I'll walk you home," he said, falling into step beside her. Kate's stomach was flipping upside down. She would swear she could feel heat emanating from of his body. He was close enough for her to slip her arm through his, but that was something she wasn't sure she should do. So they walked with their jacketed arms touching all the way back to her house.

"Listen, Kate," Adam said when they reached the front stoop. "I was on my way to your house when you stopped me. I wanted to ask you something."

Kate turned back to face him with her heart pounding.

He looked down at his shoes and said, "I wanted to ask if *you* wanted to go prom with me."

Kate's heart jumped. According to Cora and having seen him walking toward her house she expected as much, but hearing him *say* it made Kate come unglued. And seeing Adam nervous about asking her, made her chest swell with warmth.

Kate whispered, "I *want* to go with you. But Abby…"

Adam looked up at her with the eyes she adored. Again her heart stopped as she felt him look into her. It felt as if they already knew each other and had known each other for years.

"This isn't going to work out well, you know that don't you?" He asked.

She didn't care. She refused to look far ahead into the future. Right now all she needed was for Adam to take Abby to the prom and to get to North Carolina. With that thought, Kate was suddenly filled with the desire to get to North Carolina immediately. The feeling was overwhelming and impulsive. There was a 'now or never' feeling in her stomach.

"Can I go with you to North Carolina?" She blurted.

Adam stared at her, confused. Did she want to be with him or not?

"I'm getting some mixed signals here," he said.

And right then and there Kate felt the overwhelming need to tell someone the story. She needed help and she wanted it to be from

Adam. For a brief moment she wondered if he would think she was silly for going to see a psychic or that she was crazy for wanting to find out about her sister's disappearance. If he did, she would lose him before she ever even got him. But again the impulsivity coursed through her veins and she found herself telling Adam the whole story.

"I need to go to North Carolina, it's just a coincidence that you're going at the same time I need to be there," she began. "I have a sister, or had a sister, but she disappeared before I was born. My mother and I used to live in North Carolina, in Charlotte. That's where my sister disappeared from. I need to find some information about her."

"Have you tried the internet?" He asked.

Kate got the feeling he didn't want her to go. Her shoulders drooped.

"Yeah. I tried to access newspaper archives, but you have to be a resident of Charlotte in order to get a library card and you have to have the library card to get into the archives," she explained.

"Have you googled it?" He asked.

"Yep, googled it, binged it, yahooed it, everything. I've searched through a lot of missing children websites, too. I can't find anything more than I already know so I thought if I went there I might have more luck," she explained.

"So why are you just now interested?" He asked. Kate was seventeen, her sister's disappearance was twenty-one years ago.

Kate noticed how Adam picked up on the small details. She hesitated at telling him about the psychic, which is where her interest began. Her first reaction was to tell him that maybe she'd just grown curious out of the blue. She decided to test the waters instead.

"Well, see..." she started. "Abby *and* I decided we'd, for fun you know, go to see the psychic that lives on Sprit Street. We were just walking by and thought it'd be fun and, I don't know, she told me a few things and it got me curious about what happened to my sister so I decided I'd try to find out on my own."

Adam stared at her with a twisted look on his face. She imagined he'd be thinking something along the lines of *if trained detectives couldn't find her what makes you think you can find her?* Or even *seeing a psychic and buying into it? What a nutter.* Kate stood looking into his face, wondering how he'd respond.

"Well, why don't you go back there?" He asked.

"Back where?" Kate asked.

"Back to the psychic," he said. "To see if she can tell you anything more that might help."

Kate was stunned. Not only did Adam *not* think she was crazy or silly, but he was suggesting she go back to the psychic.

"Evidently she told you something that got your attention and got you thinking. Maybe you should go back and see if she can see something different or something more," he explained.

That was probably a good idea. She didn't know how she was going to come up with the forty dollars, but it might be worth it to get more information. She still couldn't get the disappointment out of her mind from Adam not wanting her to go with him to North Carolina.

Adam looked at his watch. *Oh boy,* Kate thought. *He really does think I'm nuts, he was just being polite by offering those suggestions.* Kate's heart sank. Any drop of hope she had of being with him in the future slid off her shoulder.

"It's only 7:30," he said. "Let's go pay her a visit, I'll go with you, if that's alright."

Kate was delighted at the thought of being with Adam longer, but she didn't have the forty dollars.

"I can't," Kate said. "It actually costs a lot of money."

"Oh, I wouldn't worry about that," Adam said with a new smile, a different smile. It was a smile Kate had never seen before. It was if Adam had a secret, a sneaky secret.

"It's forty dollars," she told him.

"Like I said, don't worry about it," he answered. Was he really about to pay forty dollars for a psychic reading for her?

"Adam that's too much--" she began.

"Just trust me," he interrupted. "Do you trust me?"

Kate looked at his deep brown eyes. She could still see a trace of the smile she had never seen before and then waves of shear curiosity washed over her and she *needed* to know more about her sister.

"OK," was all Kate said, and they began walking toward Sprit Street.

"So tell me what she told you the first time," Adam said.

Kate tried to remember back to that day. It was only a few days ago, but felt like a lifetime.

"It's hard to remember now," she said. She remembered the cat wrapping itself around her feet and scaring her. She remembered the old Indian lady's face and how half of it was paralyzed, but it was surprisingly not difficult to understand what she was saying. She remembered sitting in the old chair across from her and placing her hands into the lady's hands.

"She knew that I had a sister who disappeared before I was born," Kate said. "And she told me I'd lose something but gain something else." Kate realized how vague that sounded and chuckled.

But Adam didn't chuckle or smile back. In a most serious voice he asked, "What else?"

"She told me I'd go on a journey," Kate answered. It was honestly all she could remember.

Adam turned his head slightly, but not before Kate noticed the quick smile he was trying to hide. Was he laughing at her?

Kate stopped abruptly. It was fine to believe she was crazy and it was fine to not want to be around her because of it, but it was *not* OK for him to make fun of her.

"Adam, are you laughing at me?" She demanded.

Adam looked at her, his brown eyes drooping. He had not meant to make her think he was making fun of her.

"No of course not," he said.

"Because I can take care of this on my own, I don't need someone who is just going to make fun of me the whole way," she said. She was amazed at how easy it was to stand up for herself, especially to the guy she had had a crush on for almost a decade.

Adam threw up his arms saying, "whoa, whoa, whoa. Making fun of you? Kate I am not making fun of you, why would you think that?"

"Because you were smiling just now," she answered.

"I was smiling because part of her prediction has already come true. Don't you get it? A journey? Going to North Carolina with me?" He said.

So he *did* want her to go along?

"Oh," was all she could say as the pieces fell together. They began walking again.

"So I'm going then?" She asked.

"Yeah," Adam said in such a way as if to say *what else would you think?*

"How far is Queens University from Charlotte?" She asked him.

"Queens U is in Charlotte, actually," he told her.

Kate began to think about riding in his truck all the way to NC. She imagined herself sitting in the middle while he was driving. She thought his arm would be around her and they'd be listening to some love song on the radio. *That would never happen,* she thought. She remembered Abby.

"Oh," Kate said immediately. "If I'm going, let's *not* tell anyone about it though. You know, people might get the wrong idea." Adam only shook his head. He really could not figure her out. She had said she wanted to go to the prom with him, but that she wanted him to go with Abby. And now she has asked to go along on a road trip, but doesn't want anyone to even know she's spending time with him.

They turned the corner onto Sprit Street and she could see the old house looming just ahead. She noticed Adam picked up his step and she nearly had to jog to keep up with his long strides.

Adam began walking so fast that she fell behind a few steps. He walked off the sidewalk and onto the grassy lawn of the house. He was going right for the front door.

"Oh, you have to go around to the side," she said, nearly jogging to try to catch up. But Adam just kept walking. He walked right up to the steps and turned to wait for her.

"The side," she said, walking across the lawn. "We have to go to the side door."

"No we don't," Adam said. "The side door is for customers."

She climbed the steps and stood beside him.

He reached up a pointed finger as if to ring a doorbell as he said, "Family goes through the front door."

He pressed his finger to a small white spot on the brick. This confused Kate as there was no normal looking doorbell and no bell sound had been made inside the house. And yet, she could hear footsteps coming to the door.

The old Indian woman had difficulty opening the large, heavy door, but when she did she smiled at the two of them.

"I shot you'd be back," she said looking down at Kate. Then she turned to Adam and a big smile protruded out from the unparalyzed side of her face. She hugged Adam and told them to come inside.

"And how iz my seester doing?"She asked Adam.

"She's fine, she's planting a garden this year," Adam answered.

"Vould you wike some tea?" She asked.

"Yes, please," Adam answered. Then the woman looked at Kate.

"Oh no, if I drink caffeine at this time of day I'll never go to sleep," she said with a smile.

"Water zen?" She asked.

"Water would be great," Kate answered.

She had led Kate and Adam into the living room that had been just out of Kate's view the last time she had been in the house. The furniture was antique, very 1800s. Kate fell instantly in love with the style of the room. There were big, heavy portraits of men and women dressed in top hats, fancy coats, breeches and big, fluffy dresses with corsets. The fire place was ablaze and the room was warm and cozy. Small, intricate statues were on the tables. They were made of grinds and gears that were shiny gold. One was a small, miniature-sized man on an old timey tricycle where the front wheel was five times the size of the back two. The man wore a dove tailed black suit and top hat.

"Nabhanya is my aunt. Nadine, her sister, is my mother," Adam said, breaking into her thoughts.

"Nabhanya," Kate repeated. "That is very pretty."

"Zank you, dear," the lady said, reappearing from the kitchen. "Here iz your water," she said, handing Kate a bottle of ice cold water.

"Thank you," Kate said. Nabhanya and Adam began chatting and Kate returned to examining the contents of the room. She was examining an old antique lamp when she heard her name mentioned.

"…Kate to understand what she needs to look for," Adam had been saying. She had only caught the last part.

Kate looked at Nabhanya to see if she could find any annoyance in her face. But Nabhanya's face revealed nothing if she was feeling anything.

"Um, I think I should pay you, but I only have like ten dollars," Kate said.

"Zis one iz free," Nabhanya said. "I did not tell zoo too much last time. Last time zoo were on zee verge of a decision and I could not tell zoo zome zings as it would inhibit your decision. Come zit in front of me on zee carpet," she said.

Kate sat with her knees under her in front of Nabhanya and held her hands out for Nabhanya to take. But Nabhanya did not take her hands.

"I do not like to touch too much. It is difficult to do so for me. A person's past comes to fast at me when I touch," she explained. Now Kate knew why she had flinched when she took her hands before.

Kate let her arms fall to her side as Nabhanya closed her eyes and breathed in deep. She watched as Nabhanya's eyes slowly opened. Kate could see Nabhanya was not looking at her, she was not looking at anything. She was washed out. Nabhanya stared into space without blinking.

When she spoke Kate was horrified what came out. It was not Nabhanya's voice at all! This voice was dark, male and seemingly menacing.

"Look for the boy. A lake. A small car. A restaurant. A cliff. Love," the voice said. And then very quickly Nabhanya blinked and the voice was gone.

"I see zomezing for you, to help you," Nabhanya said.

"What was that?" Kate cried out, horrified. Nabhanya looked confused.

"It's called a spirit guide," Adam broke in, and then Nabhanya began to nod her head, understanding what had just happened.

"What did he zay?" Nabhanya asked.

Adam repeated the words for his aunt. Kate was so shocked she could not move. She sat still with her eyes wide open.

Nabhanya chuckled. "Don't worry, zometimes when I am tired my spirit guide will pop in. He sounds scary, but he is good," she explained.

"When you go to where your seester was taken from, you'll need to look for someone. Zis person would have been much older than your seester at zee time. He would have been zomeone that the kids all made fun of. He was not very smart and might have been developmentally delayed. He'll be able to help you. He'll be tall, around 6'4" or 6'5". He'll have a large belly, but strong arms. The zecret he holds is about your seester. Zat's who you need," she said.

Kate stared for a moment at the woman whose powers were now very real to her. There was no way this woman could have made up that voice. The voice was very masculine and very harsh.

Nabhanya stared back at Kate and then said, "Zat's all." Nabhanya slapped her hands on her knees and stood up and walked back into the kitchen.

"Make zure the door closes when you leave," she could hear Nabhanya saying as she opened a door around the corner.

Kate looked at Adam who was in the middle of a big yawn. She realized her mouth must have been gaping wide open, but she couldn't bring herself to close it. She was still in shock.

"Are you OK?" Adam asked.

Kate looked around before saying, "yeah."

"Well, let's go, it's late," he said, standing up from the chair he occupied. He was not taken aback by the creepy voice. He acted as if nothing unusual had just happened while she sat paralyzed with shock and fear.

Finally he knelt beside her and looked at her in the face.

"What you heard was a celestial being called a spiritual guide. Most, if not all, of people who have the ability to see these things, have spiritual guides. They are to help keep the bad from coming through. See there are good spirits and bad spirits. Spirit guides help keep the bad away. There are always things around us, good and bad, wanting our attention for whatever reason. Except, only very few of us are able to hear them, to see them and to understand them. People like Nabhanya have a greater chance of seeing and hearing them because her brain operates differently, like on a different frequency. That's the best way I can think to describe it anyway."

Kate tried to take it all in. She was fascinated by it. She watched Adam stroke the thick carpet as he waited for her to react. Finally he looked up at her.

"Wow." It was all she could say as she breathed out. Adam smiled at her knowingly. He stood up and offered her his hand. She took it and was taken aback at how easily it was to move. It felt like he had lifted her up all on his own, but Kate knew that couldn't be possible. He had lifted her so quickly she stood awkwardly close to him, face to face. Their noses almost touched she was so close to him.

"Sorry," she said, taking her hand from his and stepping back. But Adam only smiled as he released her hand.

On the walk home Adam explained that his whole family, as far back as they knew, was riddled with people who could see things. Everyone had some kind of ability in the psychic range. For some it was very weak, for others it was very strong. His Great Aunt, for example, could give readings even better than Nabhanya because her power was very strong. But his mother, on the other hand, couldn't do any more than tell when a cold was coming on.

"What about you?" Kate asked.

"I think I got skipped," Adam said, quite seriously.

"Nothing?" Kate asked.

"Not ever. I'm lucky I can tell when someone is upset or happy," he said with a chuckle.

"I'm really glad I saw you out the window earlier," Kate said. If she hadn't seen him, she wouldn't be going to NC and she wouldn't have revisited Nabhanya.

"In the window?" Adam asked.

"I was in the attic looking for things that might help me find something out about my sister. I looked out the window and saw you standing on the street corner," she said.

"What made you decide to come and talk to me?" He asked.

She felt stuck. She would have to give up Cora. Would Adam be mad at her?

"And how did you know I was coming to ask you to prom?" He asked, sounding as though it was the first time he had thought about it.

"Uh," Kate said. "Lucky guess?"

Adam looked down at his feet as they walked and finally it came to him. "Cora," he said. "Cora told you, didn't she?"

"Don't be mad at her," Kate said. "She told me because of Abby." Adam would never understand girls. He just hoped what he was doing was right. And for the moment, it seemed to make Kate happy so he was going with it. Adam wasn't angry at Cora anyway. He half expected her to tell Kate. But then he expected Kate would have said 'yes' to him instead of asking him to go with her friend. He wished now more than ever that he had some of his family's ancient ability so he could understand Kate.

They stood on the sidewalk in front of Kate's house. She thanked him for taking her to see his aunt to get some more information. She stood, waiting for something to happen. Kate couldn't help but think maybe there was at least a goodbye hug in store for her. After a moment, she took in a deep breath and walked away across the lawn to her front porch.

Adam lingered, watching her hand grasp the door knob. Kate waved to him before she disappeared into her house. Adam smiled and waved back, pressing himself to turn away so he could start his walk home.

CHAPTER FOUR

Kate didn't wake up until 9:30 a.m. the next day. Her mother was already awake; she could hear her in the shower. Saturday was cleaning day, which Kate actually didn't mind. Kate didn't get to see her mom much through the week because she worked at night so the weekend was really the only chance she got to see her. Her mother's bathroom was on the other side of the wall from her bathroom. When Kate was younger she would sit in the empty tub just so she could hear her mother sing as she showered. Kate smiled remembering it and decided to try it now. She slipped into the bathroom, climbed into the tub and pressed her ear against the wall. She could hear her mother mumbling, she wasn't singing. But still Kate kept her ear pressed to the wall. She sat there uneventfully, missing the sound of her mother's singing voice until she heard a buzzing noise. Kate repositioned herself to hear it more clearly. But the harder she pressed her ear to the wall, the less she heard the noise. The noise wasn't coming from her mother's side of the wall, it was coming from her bedroom. Kate jumped out of the tub and discovered her phone had buzzed so much it had fallen from her desk and was hanging by its charger cord.

She picked it up and saw that Abby had been trying to call her. She had missed calls from her that were from last night. Kate must have been sleeping hard and not heard her phone. But it was too late to answer it, it had stopped buzzing. She looked at the missed call log and saw that Abby had called her at 10:02 p.m., 10:15 p.m., and 10:49 p.m. the night before and then again a few moments ago.

Kate hit the call button and dialed three, which was the speed dial number for Abby.

"Hey, where were you last night? I kept calling and calling," she said.

"I was asleep," Kate said.

"You should take your phone off vibrate, I have some awesome news," Abby said.

Kate cradled the phone between her ear and her shoulder as she picked up her book bag to take her books out.

"Adam asked me to prom last night!" Abby said into the phone, followed by a series of squeals.

Kate wanted to squeal right along with her, but even though she knew it was going to happen, it still made her heart sink. Kate wondered what she had expected. She *told* Adam to ask Abby. She supposed she expected him to refuse to ask her. Maybe she expected him to say he wasn't going to go to prom at all if Kate wouldn't go with him. No, she hadn't expected any of those things at all. But it still hurt to know that Kate would not be the one who he was with on prom night.

"Yay!" Kate faked into the phone.

"I know!" Abby said. "We have to go to Barney's, I just know they'll have *the* dress I want."

"You already got a dress," Kate said.

"No, I need to find the perfect dress. Mini dresses are going out of style, I need something better," Abby said.

"Well, I can't go today, Mom is home," Kate told her.

"So bring her with us!" Abby said, giggling.

"I'm not so sure she'd want to go shopping with us," Kate said with a smile. "Because then she'd see how much the dresses cost and she'll have a heart attack."

"Uh oh," Abby said detecting something. "*You* haven't brought the prom up to your mom, have you?"

"No, I haven't. I was going to talk to her about it today," Kate said. And it was true; she had been planning to approach the subject with her mother soon. Today would just be that day.

"OK, but I can't wait. I have to go today. I'll text you pictures," she said. Then to Kate's dismay Abby said, "Maybe I'll ask Cora to go. You know, maybe it'll patch things up. Obviously she wasn't trying to ask Adam to prom, which I would have known if I'd just listened to her."

Yeah, that'll patch things up, Kate thought. *More like tear it down.* She guessed Abby finally talked to Cora last night and stopped ignoring her messages. She imagined Cora telling Kate that Adam had actually wanted to go with Kate. All day Kate would be worried, thinking Cora would tell Abby during their shopping trip.

"OK, but don't forget to send pics," Kate said.

"I won't," Abby said and hung up.

Quickly Kate texted Cora: 'Don't tell Abby.' She hoped Cora would know what she meant.

"Kate!" She heard her mother call from the other room.

The rest of the day Kate and her mother cleaned the house. Kate found it easy to lose herself in loads of laundry, dusting the high ceiling fans and washing down the baseboards. By noon she had worked up an appetite and they decided to have tuna fish sandwiches and potato chips. While she was munching, she heard her phone vibrate on the counter top.

Kate grabbed it up, expecting pictures of flowing designer gowns and strappy heels. But instead it was a text from a number she didn't recognize. All it said was, 'happy?'

Kate texted back, 'you got the wrong number.' She expected to receive back, 'oh I'm sorry,' or something of that nature but what she received was, 'it's me. Adam.'

Adam had her phone number. She couldn't help but smile to herself. It was her first text from him. What did 'happy?' mean though?

She texted, 'what do you mean, happy?'

"Didn't Abby tell you?" Adam asked. And then it made sense. Adam was talking about asking Abby to prom.

She texted back, 'yes and no.'

'Yes and no?' He had written back.

'Yes,' She sent.

But that only confused him more and he decided to stop while he was ahead.

The next day at school as soon as they arrived Abby was bent on finding Adam in the crowd. He was where he always was before classes started: hanging out in front of his first class. He was leaning against the wall with his hands shoved in his pockets talking to two other guys. To Kate's chagrin Abby walked up to Adam and put her arm through his and stood beside him. What was even worse, was that Adam smiled down at her and accepted the affection like it was expected. Kate stood next to Abby and drowned out their conversation as she let herself feel sorry. Abby had the guy she wanted; the only guy she had ever wanted and it was her own fault.

Adam sat next to Abby at lunch. When she had imagined him sitting at their table Kate had always imagined him sitting with her, not Abby. They were a couple now. Kate never thought it would go *that* far. She just wanted him to go to prom with Abby, not be her boyfriend. But what had she expected? It was inevitable with Abby. She had lost him.

The week was interspersed with aggravating situations where Kate had to watch them canoodling, kissing each other on the cheeks and saying sexy goodbyes. As the week wore on, her sadness took on an angry tone. Abby was completely absorbed in her new relationship and Kate was left alone to sulk much of the time. The next Sunday night she received a text from Adam. It said, 'ur still going to NC w me, rgt?'

Of course she still planned to go to North Carolina, but she had put it out of her mind because it had felt like it was forever away. She realized now that she hadn't even asked her mom if she could go. *To North Carolina? With a boy?* Kate thought. *Yeah, right.* Her mother would never go for it so she would do what anyone else would do. She would tell her mom she was staying at Abby's for the weekend and would ride to school with her on Monday. It would be the biggest lie she had ever told, but it would have to work.

'When r we leaving?' She texted back.

'Friday 8 a.m. it's a 5.5 hr drive,' the text said.

And then everything started hitting her. Where would she sleep? She'd have to rent a hotel room. How much money did she have for a hotel and food? She needed to pack. She remembered a savings account her grandmother had gotten her when she was very little; it had $500 in it. She had the account book stashed in a box under her bed. She would use it if she had to. Grabbing her wallet she found more than she expected: $45. She had a cute pink piggy bank that she dropped coins into quite often. Picking it up, she imagined it had more than a few dollars in it. But she'd have to take the change to a Coinstar. She rummaged through the kitchen drawers to find a paper bag to put the coins in. Gently she pulled back the stopper on the piggy's belly. This piggy wasn't one that had to be broken in order to get the coins. The coins spilled out and she shoveled them into the bag.

She texted, 'I'll b ready. U can pick me up?'

Adam answered, 'yes. I'll b there at 7:45.'

Perfect she thought. Her mother would still be in bed and when she woke up she'd think Kate had gone school, just like any ordinary day. Kate would tell her mother she'd be staying the whole weekend with Abby to go shopping for prom dresses.

Earlier she had talked with her mom and they had agreed that Kate could spend no more than $100 on her dress and accessories. It was a low mark, but Kate thought she could manage it. Kate thought about what she would tell Abby. Getting out of school would be easy, she'd call, pretend to be her mother and tell the office guy she was out sick for Friday. Kate hadn't missed hardly any days except earlier in the winter when she got a bad cold so she was certain it would work, but what about Abby? She'd come up with that later. Right now she needed to know how to approach the subject of where to sleep while on the trip.

She went to her laptop and began looking for hotels around Queens University. She never realized hotel rooms were so expensive, even at the cheap places. She would need $100 a night for a room. She'd need one for Friday and Saturday nights. That was the cheapest rate she could find.

She thumbed in the message, 'I found rooms at $100/night, want me to reserve u 1 as well?' She hesitated for a moment before sending it. It was awkward. She sent it anyway.

She waited for a response and finally it came. 'I got a better idea,'' the text read.

'Arthur's roommate is gone for weekend. I'll stay w him. U can stay w Arth's gf, she has apt.'

Staying with a girl I've never met before, she thought. Then she shrugged and thought, *better than parting with $200.*

'Perfect,' she texted back. Great. Good. Now she'd just have to wait a whole freaking week. The whole week she endured watching Abby and Adam again. It made her angry inside, but really she didn't understand why. It was what she wanted, wasn't it? And Abby was the happiest Kate had ever seen her. But Abby always got what she wanted. Kate noticed a big decline in phone calls from Abby at night. She imagined it was because she was on the phone with Adam. By the time Friday came around, she was so angry that she almost decided she wouldn't go, but she had to. She had still not been able to find any other information about her sister all week. All she found were new places on the web that had the same information.

CHAPTER FIVE

By the time Adam showed up outside her house at 7:40 a.m. in an old red pickup truck she had ruminated on the situation so much that she was seething with anger, but she was determined not to let it show. She had packed her book bag with a jump suit and t-shirt and a pair of jeans with a thick sweater. She figured they would be comfortable for wandering around the city. She left wearing a pink hoodie over a small t-shirt and jeans. She brought along her heavy jacket, too, just in case it got really cold. The weather was supposed to warm up the next week. Before she left she had checked the weather and the weekend was supposed to be a cold one.

She opened the passenger side door, threw her bag in and jumped up into the seat.

"Mornin'," Adam said.

"Mornin'," was all Kate could muster.

Adam pulled the truck out of the driveway and started down the road. They were quiet for some time. He told Kate he had told Abby all about going to see Arthur, but decided to leave out the part that Kate was going along with him.

"So do you know where you're going to start?" Adam said eventually.

"No. No I don't," Kate said with frustration in her voice.

"Are you OK?" Adam asked.

"Yeah," Kate said quickly.

"You seem kind of upset," he said.

For a moment Kate thought about telling him how she felt; how angry she was at him. But she couldn't find the logic in being angry at him so she knew it was unfair. The impulsiveness rose up in her and she had to fight to keep it at bay. She wanted so bad to tell him how angry she was at him.

"I think I'm just tired," she answered.

"Did you eat breakfast, do you want to stop somewhere?" He asked.

She looked over at him and her anger melted away. His profile was perfect. His dark hair was cut shorter with tiny spikes on the top. It glistened with dried gel. His arms were covered by the perfect shade of dark brown, crushed leather. His lips were plump and slightly pink. His skin was not as caramel colored as

Nabhanya's. It was not white either. It was somewhere in between. And even though they weren't looking at her, she could imagine the sweet look in his eyes. His hands were perhaps her favorite thing in the world. They were strong and masculine and thinking of having them around her made her smile slightly.

"You got a haircut," she said.

"Yeah, it's kind of short," Adam said, carefully patting the spikes on top.

"I like it," Kate said. He turned to look at her and smiled. She smiled back him. Her hair was long and dark. A silver beret held it out of her eyes. The curls that slid down her back were perfect and images of waking up entangled in them were flashing through Adam's mind.

Immediately he turned back to face the road. He wouldn't let himself think about those things.

"No, I ate before we left. I have a breakfast bar if you want it," she said, answering his question.

"That's OK, I ate too," he said.

Then they were back to awkward silence. He hadn't thought about how he would fill the five and half hour drive with conversation.

Now that Kate was past her anger for the moment, she found it a little easier to be sociable. She talked to Adam about their baseball season, his friend Carl and how he needed a date to the prom –hint hint- about the weather, their teachers and everything else, except Abby. Neither one of them brought her up in conversation.

When they arrived at campus Adam parked on a side street just off of campus parking. Parking on campus required a parking pass.

"Hey, it's me. We're on La--" Adam said. He had called his brother and was trying to pronounce the name of the street they were on.

"La roose," Kate said, pronouncing La Raouse for him.

"La roose street," Adam told his brother.

After a few 'uh-huhs' and 'yeps' Adam hung up the phone and shoved it back in his pocket. The truck was still running.

"Celia lives on Bucknell Rd., it's just around the corner, he said he'll meet us there," Adam told her. Abby assumed Celia was

Arthur's girlfriend. Adam put the truck in gear and rolled back out onto the street. They made a few turns and Kate saw the white letters on the green sign, 'Bucknell Road.' Adam was looking out the window, counting houses and murmuring directions under his breath. Finally they pulled into the parking lot of a series of tall two-story townhouse buildings.

"1504," Adam said with satisfaction. He undid the seatbelt and opened his door. Kate did the same.

They walked together to the front door and rang the bell. Kate saw a curtained window with a soft light flowing through it. She could make out the profile of a tall, slim lamp and the back of a couch just inside.

"Coming!" They heard someone inside yell.

A half out of breath small figured girl opened the door. She was smaller than Kate, with wispy light brown, mousy hair. She wore eye glasses that were very thick. She smiled up at Kate and Adam.

"Come in, sorry. I am running late, I have class in a half hour so I got to go, but please, make yourselves at home," she said.

She opened the door wide and as Kate and Adam made their way in, the girl shuffled past them with a large backpack.

"Arthur will be here soon," she said, shutting the door behind her in in a hurry. A few moments later they heard a car start up and actually squeal tires when leaving the parking lot.

Kate sat on the couch. Adam took out his phone and began texting. Kate guessed he was texting Arthur. Afterward he came to sit on the couch too. It was a nice couch. It was light brown and soft. As Kate looked around she realized that the girl had very nice furniture. There was a real honest-to-goodness Tiffany's lamp on a side table. Mahogany seemed to be a theme. Behind the rich entertainment shelving was a staircase. There was nothing special about it, just a carpeted staircase with a wood banister.

"So, do you have a date to prom?" Adam asked, interrupting her viewing.

"Oh, um, no," Kate said. She hadn't really even thought about it. She knew prom should be the most important thing on her mind, but it wasn't. She didn't grow up fantasizing about prom or getting married, having a wedding or kids. She knew most girls did, but she did not. There was something more pressing on her mind than a silly dance.

Good, Adam thought. He didn't want anyone to take Kate to the prom. The thought of someone else dancing with her, standing close to her, feeling her breath on them…it nearly enraged him. *Jealousy*, he thought. *This must be what jealousy is.*

Adam looked over at Kate, who was looking around the room. He looked down at her hand, pressed against the cushion of the couch. It was a light brown color, very tan, especially for February. On her middle finger was a small, thin gold ring. Somehow he knew it had come from her mother. It must have been a gift. Maybe it was something handed down, a small heirloom of sorts. Adam didn't know how he knew it; he just seemed to know it and he found that curious.

"I don't think I'll go," Kate said, still looking around the room.

"You have to go," Adam started.

"I'm not really into it. I know I'm supposed to be, but…I don't know. I'm just not," she tried to explain.

"You have to go," Adam said again. This time he added, "you said you'd save me a dance."

Kate smiled to herself and looked at Adam, who smiled back at her.

Kate felt bad for wanting to sit closer to him. Instantly in her mind she flashed scenes of them kissing on the couch, in the truck or standing outside. And then, as always, there was Abby's face and the whole imagery would dissipate.

Adam noticed Kate's face drop. He imagined she was thinking too much about finding more information about her sister's disappearance. He could tell it was very troubling for her, but it brought her to NC with him. That was all that mattered. She was there.

There was a knock at the door. Adam jumped up quickly and opened it. It was Arthur.

Kate stood up to say hello. Arthur had grown taller since she saw him last year. When he left high school he was nearly a foot shorter than Adam. Now he was slightly taller than Adam. Arthur was much skinnier than Adam, dorky-looking even. He had the same dark hair, the same color skin, the same dark eyes, but Adam had something that Arthur was missing. Arthur was the smart kid, the one who knew the answer to all the hard chemistry problems. Adam was a dreamer, a thinker. If Arthur were the Forensics Leader, Adam was the FBI agent. Arthur was in the lab, Adam was in the field.

"So what did you guys have in mind to do today?" Arthur asked.

"I need a library," Kate said quickly. Perhaps she said it too quickly.

Arthur looked at Kate with amusement. A smile trickled across his lips and he said, "A library?"

Adam explained, "Kate is looking for some…" he paused for a moment on the realization that what Kate was looking for was a secret. Perhaps because no one else in Change Modei seemed to know about what happened to Kate's sister or that Kate even had a sister, or perhaps it was the way in which Kate had told him the story, but something clued him in on the fact that this was Kate's secret. Somehow he had always known it was a secret for her. He wondered how he knew it.

"Information about newspapers," he finished slowly and carefully. "For a report she's doing," he added. Then he nodded and smiled, satisfied with his instant lie.

Kate smiled back at him for not revealing the real reason she needed the library.

"Well, alright then. You'll want the Charlotte Mecklenburg County Library. I'll take you there," Arthur said.

Arthur turned and opened the door he had just come in through. Adam held the door open for Kate who smiled as she walked past him. Briefly she indulged in the heat emanating from his body, just like the walk they shared to and from her house pre-Abby. This time she caught a sniff of his cologne. She recognized it as Ralph Lauren Polo Black. For a moment she closed her eyes to commit it to memory.

"The Mecklenburg should have what you need. It has a very expansive collection, I've found them quite handy on a number of occasions," Arthur reported. Kate thought he spoke very eloquently. She imagined him playing the part of Ducky on NCIS. He would make a good younger version of a Ducky.

On the drive to the library Kate sat in the back seat of Arthur's old Ford Focus and thought about how odd of a family she had come across while Arthur's chattering faded into the background. She had known Adam and Arthur for over a decade and known nothing of their family until two weeks ago. She began to think about what their mother might be like. She imagined her to be tall for a woman, slender and very organized. She remembered the features of the Native American psychic who was Adam's aunt, but couldn't put any of her physical traits in line with her image of Adam and Arthur's mother. She imagined their mother to be soft and sweet and caring with slight features, small and perfectly proportioned. She imagined their mother would be the type to have cookies made for an after school snack.

Kate's thoughts came crashing down around her as the car they were in came to a sudden stop. Her arms flopped up as her cheek smashed against the back of the front passenger seat. She let out a series of groans as she heard a loud 'pop' come from the back end of the vehicle.

"Sorry, it does that sometimes, it's just backfiring" Arthur said. "But we're here. It isn't too far from campus."

"Great," Kate said, grabbing up her book bag and purse. "I'll call you when I'm finished." Despite the pain in her jaw, Kate quickly opened the door and walked hurriedly toward the front entrance of the library.

The large building loomed just ahead of her. It looked a little outdated with the light brown brick and tinted glass. She didn't know if she'd be able to find what she was looking for inside or not.

As she walked through the doors the smell of old book glue filled her nose. She had entered the world of fantasy, forbidden loves, vampires, werewolves, leprechauns, and all the demons of the night. She loved the smell of old books. Just ahead was a semi round desk, behind which the library workers floated back and forth.

She must have been staring in awe at the size of the library because one of the ladies raised her head from the book she held in her hands and asked, "May I help you?"

Kate knew she wouldn't be able to get much of anywhere without a library card, but she asked anyway, "I'm looking for the microfilms."

The lady smiled, put her book down on the counter and began walking toward a back room. Kate followed her and when the lady motioned for her to sit in a seat in front of the machine she was more than happy to do so.

"I'm looking for microfilm from the Charlotte Observer from 1993. The months of May and June…I think," Kate said.

"That's quite a large span. Anything in particular you're looking for?" The lady asked.

"Articles on a disappearance, a girl named Loraine Margaret Cooper from Charlotte," Kate answered.

The lady stared at her for a moment. Kate looked up into her face to see the same sadness she would see in her mother's eyes when she did something to disappoint her.

"I remember that," the woman said. "It was a very long time ago. The whole town was looking for her. Did you know her?"

Kate hesitated at revealing her identity, but wondered if the woman knew anything more than she did about the disappearance.

"She's my sister," Kate said, decidedly.

The sadness in the woman's eyes turned to sorrow and her brow furrowed further.

"I should have known. You look so much like her. She used to come here every Saturday when she was young for our children's reading day. She must have been about your age when she disappeared," the woman said.

Kate wanted to tell her she was off by four years, but there were more important things to ask. She wondered how anyone could remember anyone considering the size of the library. The children's reading days must have been filled with dozens of kids.

"She was fourteen. Did she come alone? Did she ever come with a friend?" Kate asked.

"Well, with your mother of course. But not any other kids," the lady said.

"Were you always here on Saturdays? Would there be someone else who might have been around when she would come in? Someone else who might would remember her, too?" Kate asked.

"Back then I was the reader for children's reading day, so it was always me. As for anyone else having known her, I wouldn't know. Carol might have been working here back then, but she's not here today," the lady said. Then she turned and walked away abruptly. Kate wondered if she had asked one too many questions.

Kate sat the machine for a few minutes, off thinking about all the questions she had about her sister. But soon the woman came back with several slides and fished out the ones she thought might have articles with information about Loraine. Kate examined them thoroughly but four films later, she was getting impatient. On the fifth film she saw a mention of her sister in the briefs. She read the article quickly, sifting through information she already had and then something new popped up; the name of a Detective who had taken the case: Detective Jack Morrow. Kate pulled out her small notebook from her pocket and wrote the name down. It gave her hope so she continued looking through every single slide, doing so carefully so as not to miss anything. Several more films later she was still empty handed. There were many articles chronicling the search for her sister. It was a search the whole neighborhood had participated in, but no one ever found a single clue as to her sister's disappearance.

After two hours and countless articles, Kate had found three new pieces of information:

1.   Detective Jack Morrow had been assigned to the case.
2.   Loraine disappeared from 123 Goodwin Avenue on June 3, 1993.
3.   Loraine had been wearing a blue cotton t-shirt, light-colored jeans and a thin, gold ring.

Kate looked down at her hand. The thin, gold ring on her left middle finger shined bright. Her mother had bought it for her on her fourteenth birthday. She remembered her mother coming to sit on her bed beside her and telling her what it meant to be a woman. She gave her the ring "as a rite of passage." She could hear her mother's voice saying the words, making her feel proud, scared and awkward all at the same time.

Kate looked at her phone, it was 4:00 p.m. and the library would be closing in a half hour. She dialed Adam's number and listened as it rang five times until finally going to voicemail. *Great, I hope he remembers me soon*, she thought before leaving him a voicemail.

"Hey, it's me, Kate. Come get me when you can. I'll start walking to the apartment from here, pick me up along the way," she said quietly into the phone.

Kate sighed as she looked at all the films that were scattered around her. The woman from earlier had gotten them all for her so she didn't know where they went. Off to her right she spotted a cart that said, 'microfilms' on it. It only had two other films on it, but she assumed it was where the used ones were supposed to go so a library worker could put them in the right spot somewhere else.

Kate gathered up the films and unloaded them onto the cart. One film fell off and as she bent to pick it up, she saw a sign on the opposite wall, 'internet.' Below was a series of computers and nearly every one of them was empty. She knew there would be no ability to use the computers without a library card. After putting the film back on the cart and making sure it was secure she scooted over to the computers to make sure. Kate plopped down in the seat and hit the space bar to bring one computer out of sleep mode. The computer prompted Kate to sign in using her library card number. Kate slumped down in the seat. She desperately wanted to be able to leave the library with a phone number for Detective Morrow.

She glanced to her left and saw a small boy typing faster than she'd ever seen anyone type. His back was straight and his feet were crossed. He wore thin rimmed glasses and had sandy blonde hair. She watched him type an emphatic period, sit back in the seat with his arms crossed and reread what he had just written. The look on his face was one of satisfaction. She watched him save his work and eject his USB memory stick from the side of the monitor. His book bag lay beside him and he picked it up with great difficulty after standing. Kate guessed him to be about twelve. She noticed his light colored khaki pants were about an inch too short. She watched him limp away with the heaviness of the bag before she suddenly realized that it was her chance.

She hurried over to where the boy had sat, nearly knocking over a chair as she went. She pressed the space bar as soon as her hand could reach it, to save it from going into sleep mode where she'd have to sign in. She caught it just in time. The computer was still logged in under the boy's card number. Oh how she loved it when people forgot to sign out.

She ignored the written work the boy had done inside a Microsoft word document and quickly opened a browser. She searched google first and found a phone number within the first few hits. She scribbled it down in her notebook next to the detective's name.

Her phone rang. Digging it out of her pocket she saw that it was Adam.

"Hey, sorry I didn't answer earlier, I didn't hear the phone ring," he shouted into the phone. In the background she heard the huffs, grunts and chants of a dozen deep male voices. Then suddenly she heard the uproar of all the men.

"We're watching the football game," he yelled. "We'll be there to get you in fifteen minutes."

"OK," Kate said a little too loud. The few people who were still left in the library all gave her stern looks.

She hung up the phone and noticed she had a few text messages. There were three, all from Adam. She had gotten caught up in the task at hand and hadn't paid any attention to her phone. The texts were all asking her if she was almost finished, telling her they wanted to go watch the football game and asking if she wanted to go, too.

Kate felt bad for missing the texts and interrupting their game. She was already a nuisance in Adam's life and now Arthur probably didn't have a keen liking for her either. She realized she might have come off as a little rude to ask to be taken the library the first thing. But she couldn't help it, she didn't have much time, and it was, after all, what she had come for.

CHAPTER SIX

Kate sat on the steps of the library that had closed almost a half hour ago. She was freezing and still waiting for Adam and Arthur to show up to take her back to Celia's apartment. The street had grown quiet and the sun was beginning its descent into the horizon.

Her jaw had stopped pulsing hours ago, but now her neck was sore from craning into the microfilm machine for hours. She rolled her neck around, closed her eyes and tried to concentrate on the relaxation breathing techniques she had learned in gym class. She was still sitting with her eyes closed when she heard a vehicle stop just a few yards in front of her. It was Adam.

As she jumped into the passenger side, she realized Arthur wasn't with him.

"I'm so sorry," she began, apologizing. "I had my phone volume turned down low because, well, because I was in a library. I was so engrossed that I didn't even *look* at it for hours. I totally interrupted your football game, I'm so sorry."

To her relief Adam only smiled at her as he put the truck in gear.

"Actually, I'm really glad you did," he said. "I'm not particularly into football. Baseball I'll watch, but not football. I've never been a football fan. That was always dad and Arthur's thing."

Kate wondered if he was only telling her that so she wouldn't feel bad. Though it might sound sweet, it annoyed Kate. She did not like the thought of Adam telling her something just because he thought it was what she would want to hear, but maybe he was being truthful. She couldn't remember him ever *going* to a football game. Both Kate and Abby had been on the cheerleading team until their sophomore year of high school. Thinking back on it, Kate realized how much work it had been to be a cheerleader.

"You don't like football, do you?" Adam asked, uncertain.

"I used to," Kate answered honestly. "Before it consumed my world. Now I can't stand it."

She could see Adam beginning to remember her previous cheerleading status.

A curious look crossed his face as he asked, "why *did* you stop cheerleading?"

The answer was complicated. Abby had been eyeing the spot for Team Captain, but so had Kate. While Abby had the looks and the perfect stomach, Kate had fluid movements and perfect athletic flips. She had overheard the coach and the assistant coach discussing who should get Captain. Their conversation led her to believe Kate was the obvious choice. Kate was obviously a better leader, but Abby was the stereotype. Kate saw this issue and to date wondered if Abby had ever even noticed the impending problem. So Kate began saying she wanted to quit because she was too old to be doing it. She needed to concentrate on her SAT's and honors classes to get ready for college. Her coaches tried diligently to change her mind, but she kept firm about her decision and next season Abby was made captain. The team kept it no secret that they were angry at Kate for quitting. They taunted her often about deserting them. But Kate just kept her attention on SAT scores. Abby was captain and there had been no issue to tear them apart. She still grappled with the decision, wondering if it had been the best thing to do. Being cheerleading captain would have looked fabulous on her resumes and college applications. Quitting did not.

"I just didn't feel it in me to cheer anymore," Kate said. She felt like perhaps it had fit her strange transformation over the past few years. Recently she had grown more inward, less involved with the community around her. She found herself spacing out in classes she once had actually enjoyed. She found herself dreaming of her life once she was out of high school.

Adam *had* noticed the change in Kate. He could remember a time when Kate had been just as bubbly as Abby. But lately he noticed how Kate didn't smile often, didn't laugh as freely and how distant she had become. Now that he was thinking on it, he wondered if it had anything to do with Kate's sister's disappearance. Perhaps Kate had only just recently learned about it. Somehow Adam knew that wasn't true. There was something in the way Kate held herself when she first told Adam about Loraine. He couldn't put his finger on how he knew, but he just knew that Kate had known about her sister for a long time. Why was it only just now bothering her? Why the sudden interest in a sister that was lost long ago? But Kate had already told him the answer to that question. Nabhanya.

"Did you find anything?" He asked Kate.

Kate looked at him confused, not understanding what he was talking about at first. Then she remembered.

"Oh, um, yeah I found the name of a detective," she answered.

"That's a good start," he said.

"I think he still works around here, too, I found his number on google," she explained.

"Are you going to look for him tomorrow?" Adam asked.

Kate wanted to go the precinct right away. But she couldn't imagine asking Adam to take her there now.

"Yeah," Kate answered, and then asked, "Where are we going?"

Adam couldn't figure out how he knew it, but he felt very strongly that Kate wasn't being up front with him. There was something she was holding back. He glanced over at her to see her staring out the passenger window and the feeling grew stronger. His mind began to reel, thinking of what he must be missing. Why was he suddenly so connected to the world around him? He filled his thoughts of Kate, her hair and the way it smelled when she walked by him. The small noises she made when she slept for the last few hours of the ride down. The way she always looked so concentrated, so disconnected. He ran his mind through what she might have seen in the films…police reports, articles, maps. Finally it came to him.

"Do you want to go to the police station right now?" He didn't know how he did it. He just somehow knew it was what she wanted.

Kate turned her head quickly to him. He noticed the surprise in her eyes at how he knew what she wanted.

"What about the game?" She asked. She hoped that by asking a second time that he'd slip and reveal he really wanted to see the game if he did.

But he said simply and with a scowl, "I'm not particularly into football."

"How'd you do that?" Kate asked.

"Do what?" Adam asked.

"Read my mind," Kate answered.

Adam thought for a moment. He hadn't read her mind at all. He only pieced things together. Hadn't he? But what was that strange sensation in the first place; the feeling of knowing there was something more that Kate wasn't telling him?

"I didn't," Adam said slowly.

"Then how did you know I wanted to go look for the detective right now?" She asked.

"I didn't. I guessed," he stuttered. "I mean, if it were me, I'd want to know right away." *That sounds reasonable,* Adam thought. And it was true; he would have wanted to know everything right away.

"Oh," Kate said, shrinking into the seat. She suspected perhaps Adam hadn't been completely truthful when he told her he had not inherited any of his aunt's ability to foresee things. She wondered if maybe he did in fact have some ability, however miniscule it might be.

"Is your phone a smart phone?" Adam asked.

"Yeah," she said. She dug the phone out of her pocket.

"Go online and see if you can find an address for the police station," Adam said. But Kate was already on it.

"East Seventh Street," she said. "That's not far from here, but maybe I should call ahead and make sure that's the station he is at because I also found a sheriff's office."

Adam parallel parked on the street and opened the glove box. He took out the GPS system he had used to get to Charlotte and searched for the station on East 7th Street.

"You're right, it isn't far at all. It's just around the corner," he said.

Kate was dialing the phone number.

"Hi, may I speak with Detective Morrow?" Kate asked.

Adam was pulling out into traffic again.

"Oh," he heard Kate say in a disappointed tone.

"OK, thank you," he heard.

Kate let out a big sigh.

"What?" Adam asked.

"He's retired. He retired three years ago," Kate said.

Now Adam sighed. He turned into a large empty parking lot and stopped the vehicle.

"Well, all businesses have human resource files on their employees. I bet there are some files somewhere that would give his home address or at least a phone number," Adam said. The words just tumbled out of his mouth. He had no intention of trying to *find* the files, he was just rambling, but Kate was desperate.

"Let's go then. We'll go inside and try to find the files," Kate said.

Adam chuckled.

"I don't think we could do that," he said.

"Why not?" Kate asked.

"Because it's a police station," Adam said, matter-of-factly.

"So," Kate said, shrugging her shoulders.

"What? Are you planning on creating a distraction and--" Adam started.

"Yeah," Kate interrupted. "We'll go in, see what things are like, see if we can locate the files and then we'll wait for something big to happen and I'll just go right in," she said.

"Kate--" Adam began. He wanted to explain to her how unlikely that was to happen, but then she turned to him.

"Let's at least check it out," she said.

Adam couldn't argue with that. He expected that when they got there Kate would realize what a sorry plan she had and want to try something different.

Adam drove into the public parking area beside the station and found a spot. He hadn't even put the truck in park all the way but Kate was already opening her door and walking briskly along the side of the building. Adam jumped out and trotted to catch up with her.

They walked through the front doors of the building and quickly saw the place was dead empty. The Charlotte police station was empty on a Friday night? They looked at each other confused.

From somewhere in the back they heard a voice yelling and knew that it was a female officer. Quickly Kate ran to the desk and ducked down low. From the other side of the desk, if the officer came into the lobby, they would not be able to see her.

"What can I do for you?" The woman shouted out to Adam, who was standing in the middle of the lobby still.

"Uhm," he said. His brain would not work. He could not think of a single thing to ask, nothing came to him.

"Are you here to pick someone up?" The woman growled loudly.

"No," Adam managed.

"Are you here to post bail for someone?" She asked, putting her hand on her hip.

"No," Adam said.

"Then what do you need?" The woman asked harshly.

"Uhm, I was wondering if you could tell me how I would be able to contact a retired detective."

Kate had been holding her breath and now she released it. It wasn't the best distraction, but perhaps it would give her enough time.

"Well, I might could, but you'll need to tell me first why you got a girl sneaking around under the desk," the woman said.

Kate's breath caught again. How in the world did she know?

Adam looked at the woman, thinking the same thing.

"I said," the woman had leaned over the counter and was yelling in Kate's ear. "What are you doing down there?"

Kate jumped up and spun around to face the woman.

"I'm sorry," Kate said. She didn't know what exactly she was apologizing for, but it seemed fitting.

"For what?" The woman asked. "What are you doing?"

"We just wanted to know if you could give us an address for Detective Jack Morrow," Kate asked.

"Well I might have, but you're in here being all sneaky and shit and I don't like the sneaky," she said.

"Why don't you tell me why you're really here?" She demanded.

"Really, that's why we're here," Adam interjected, stepping forward to stand beside Kate.

"We're looking for a way to contact Detective Morrow," he said.

The woman looked from Adam to Kate and then back to Adam. She raised her finger and pointed first at Adam, then at Kate and back to Adam.

"I don't like the sneaky," she said again. "You two go sit right over there in those two chairs where I can see you both. Don't you move. I'll get you a phone number. If either one of you tries anything sneaky I'm going to put you in a holding cell until your mommy or daddy comes to get you, understand?"

"Yes," Adam and Kate answered together.

They shuffled to the chairs and watched the woman go into the back room again.

"How did she know I was there?" Kate asked.

"Cameras," Adam said, pointing to a camera mounted just above the entrance and focused right at the desk. Next to it was a TV screen that showed in real time what the camera was recording.

Kate felt pretty stupid. Of course a police station would have cameras everywhere.

In the back they could hear the woman talking roughly to someone on the phone. They couldn't make out what she was saying, but she was obviously good at her job. She didn't seem to take any shit from anyone.

After about five more minutes the woman came back out to the front desk with a yellow sticky note.

"Here's a number you can reach him at, but good luck. The last I heard he was overseas, travelling to Greece or somewhere like that," she said. Kate walked up to the desk and retrieved the sticky note.

"Thank you," she said, looking down at the note. There were two numbers on it. One was a local number and the second one was an international number.

"Is this a number in Greece?" She asked.

The woman looked at her, shook her head and said, "Do I look like I know? Now go home, kids. It's getting late, you don't want to be out in downtown when it's late like this. My grandma always said, ain't nothing good happen on the streets after midnight."

Kate dug her phone out of her pocket again; she looked at the clock on it. It was only 5:30 p.m., the sun hadn't even set yet. But she had what she needed and so they walked out the front door.

As they entered the cold evening air, Kate was reminded to be embarrassed about not thinking about cameras. She felt even more embarrassed since all they had to do was ask for the stupid address to get it.

They turned the corner of the building and could see Adam's truck ahead. Kate walked to the passenger side and was startled when she realized Adam was on her side as well. He unlocked her door and opened it for her. She smiled to herself and thanked him as she climbed into the cab. She relished in the fact that he had opened the door for her twice. Adam was nearly to his door before she thought to reach over and unlock it for him.

He jumped into the driver's seat and turned the ignition key. The truck started right up and he cranked the heat.

He rubbed his hands together and then turned to face Kate.

She sat looking at him until the awkwardness set in.

"What?" She asked, feeling dreamy.

"Well aren't you going to call him?" He asked.

Kate felt stupid again and her cheeks blushed.

"Oh, right," she said, digging out the phone.

She punched in the local number and sat listening to it ring. It rang five times before an answering machine picked up the call. But Kate didn't leave a message, she hung up the phone. To her dismay she realized she was going to have to pay for an international phone call.

"You don't have international calling do you?" She asked Adam.

"No one answered?" He asked.

"Nope. It's just my luck that he's not even in the United States," she said.

"Maybe he's just out, it's Friday night," Adam said, taking Kate's phone from her hand.

She watched as he hit redial and waited the five rings.

"This is Adam Yanso, I'm calling to ask you some questions about a case you had in 1993. If you could, call me back at 604-775-8080 or at 604-775-0373."

Adam hung the phone up and handed it to Kate. Kate smiled to herself. She liked it when Adam took charge and made things happen. Well, probably nothing would happen of the phone call, at least not in the next few months. She probably wouldn't receive a return call when they came home from overseas and got the voicemail…and that's when it hit her. She remembered she and her mother went on a month long vacation to Maine in the summer. When they returned home, there were so many messages on the machine that it was full. But they were so accustomed to getting their voicemails on their cell phones that they didn't even bother to check the house phone's answering machine until one of her mother's friends at work had told her that she'd been trying to reach her. The home phone was the only phone number she had for her mother. She was trying to tell her that their good friend had given birth to her baby. So since the detective's answering machine wasn't full, perhaps they *weren't* overseas. A new sense of hope filled her.

"Well, just in case they *are* gone, we should probably think of another way to get information," Adam said.

Kate looked at him. He had said, 'we' meaning the two of them, together.

"What about Arthur?" Kate asked.

"What about him?" Adam said, confused.

"Well, I mean, you came here to see him. Wouldn't he be a little upset if you spent most of your time with me; helping me with a 'report'?" She said.

"Nah," Adam said. "He won't mind." But Adam wondered if Kate might be right. He could feel inside of himself that Kate was not going to be cautious in the endeavor. He understood that Kate was going to find what she needed to find. What if it led her to a serial killer? What if *she* disappeared? The weight of the dangerousness of the situation began to weigh heavy on him. He knew if he let her do it alone, that something bad would happen to her. He didn't know *how* he knew it, he just did.

She didn't want Arthur to be upset with Adam. She knew she could handle finding information on her own, but it would be nice to have someone to help her. And it'd be even more nice to have *Adam* help her. Selfishness won out and so Kate sat silently.

"I know!" Kate blurted out, startled by her own sudden thought. "I can google the phone number and see if I can get an address to match it."

Adam continued to drive.

After five minutes of searching for the information Kate was empty-handed.

"They all want you to sign up for an account and pay a monthly fee to get that information," she said.

"Did you try whitepages.com?" He asked.

Kate's fingers typed in the web address and she put the information into the required fields to do a reverse phone number look up.

"Hey I got something," she said. "It says Chestnut Lane. It doesn't give a house number though. It says Margaret Morrow, Race Morrow and Johnathan Morrow."

"No Jack?" Adam asked.

"Jack is the diminutive form of Johnathan," Kate explained.

"You're throwing big words at me," Adam said with a chuckle.

Kate smiled and said, "Diminutive means 'smaller version of'."

"Who names their kid Race?" He asked.

"I don't know," Kate said, shrugging. She was busy locating Chestnut Lane on her phone.

"It's about twenty-five minutes from here," Kate said.

"Should we go to the neighborhood where she disappeared from? You know, look around, see what we can see and ask the neighbors some questions?" Adam suggested.

"Yeah. But it's almost seven. No one likes it when strangers at the door interrupt their dinner or wake their kids. Plus, I'm starving," Kate said.

"Me too. Want Moe's?" He asked.

"Yeah, that sounds really good."

Adam found the restaurant in his GPS and they made the twenty minute trip across town.

"So tomorrow," Adam said with a mouth full of burrito, "we'll start at that house. We'll ask the neighbors if they lived there during that time and who the other neighbors were that moved away."

Kate stared at Adam's ravenous eating. She never thought she'd ever be disgusted by Adam Yanso, but today was that day. Lettuce and shredded cheese flew out of his mouth with each big bite and her stomach turned. Her own burrito lay unwrapped. She peeled the wrapping away slowly, letting her fingers wrap around the soft tortilla. It was warm and so it warmed her hands. If she weren't so hungry, she would have lost her appetite, but she was starving. She closed her eyes and bit in, trying to think of something other than watching Adam eat.

Adam swallowed with one big gulp and Kate wondered if he even chewed it.

"Oh and we'll have to ask about a boy that everyone picked on. That's the important part, I think," he said.

Kate had forgotten all about that. She was certainly glad Adam was there, gross eating habits or not. He was good at keeping her focused.

"What about Arthur?" She asked again.

Adam looked down at the bite of burrito he had left in his hand. His brows furrowed and he pinched his lips up on one side of his mouth.

"Would you want him to help us?" He asked.

Kate thought for a moment. There was really no reason she wouldn't want to tell Arthur. She trusted him, just as she trusted Adam. And Arthur lived very far from where she lived with her mother, so really who could he tell that would cause the secret to get around town? *Oh, only everyone he graduated with*, she thought. Perhaps it would be best to keep Arthur out of it.

"I could tell him not to talk about it, that's it's your secret," Adam said. For a second time he had read her mind.

"How do you *do* that?" She asked.

This time Adam was confident that he was able to read Kate. He wasn't reading her mind; he was simply able *feel* what she wanted. He had never been able to do it with anyone else. Not even Abby, who he'd grown close to in the past few weeks. He felt a strange connection to Kate, like in some other life they might have been together, if past lives existed.

"I'm not sure," he said. "It just comes to me with you. Somehow I know."

Kate smiled, "well, maybe you inherited more of your family's abilities than you think."

Why didn't he consider that? It was an interesting solution. Perhaps Kate was right.

"I don't know Arthur well, do you think he'd do that?" She asked.

"Oh yeah, Arthur is the best secret keeper, trust me," he said with that rare smile she had seen the night they visited his aunt.

She did trust him and she felt deep inside she could trust Arthur as well.

"You didn't eat much," Adam said.

Kate looked down at her plate and saw she'd only taken one bite out of her burrito. She picked it up and took a few more bites.

Back in the truck Adam took out his phone. The light from the screen coming out of sleep mode lit up the truck.

"It's only 7:15, the game wouldn't be over by now," he said.

"Maybe we should go, you know, to show our faces and be polite," Kate suggested.

"Well," Adam said. "I *really* don't like football."

Kate chuckled.

"Then I guess we can go to the apartment," Kate said. That would be an awkward situation, alone in an apartment together. She could see Adam's face go straight and serious as he considered it.

"Kate," he said, looking at her with a serious face. "You know I still like you, don't you?"

Kate looked straight ahead, out the front window.

"Yes," she said. She wanted to tell him she liked him, too. Somehow her interest in Abby's happiness was starting to take a backseat to her desire for him. Sitting there she could feel his warmth. He was always so warm. She could smell the faint scent of cologne. She remembered all the dreams she had had over the years; dreams of his fingertips brushing her cheeks, their foreheads together, his arms wrapped around her. When she was in middle school she would dream of him kissing her at a dance, or in the woods, or at the mall. Recent years she'd dreamt of him holding her, lying in bed together. Kissing and touching and feeling; she would dream of his hands cupping her breast, his fingers running through her hair.

Kate realized her breath had gotten heavy. "I know, but Abby."

"Abby's great, she really is," he said and Kate's heart dropped. "She's smart, she's funny, and she's really pretty, but there's something about you, Kate. I'm not sure what it is, but it's you that I want to be with."

She sat there, listening to the words she'd only dreamt of hearing. How did it come to this? How did they get to this point? Was it really happening? Kate's eyes filled with tears that she refused to let go of. She would not cry, not matter how bad her heart was hurting at the moment.

"Kate," he said and paused. "Do you...have any feelings at all for me?" He asked. She turned her head toward him and caught his eyes unexpectedly. She could feel the hurt in his eyes, the longing and she wondered if his heart was hurting like hers.

"Yes," she said. After a moment she added, "I always have."

"Then why this business with Abby?"

Kate realized the inevitable. She could not continue forward without having Adam for herself, and she knew what it meant for Abby. Abby would be crushed, but if she didn't, it would just end up like cheerleading. She would take the backseat again. Was this going to continue to happen in her life? Would she always be standing aside so Abby could have the life she wanted?

"I thought I could try to not like you anymore, for Abby. She just..." Kate tried, but couldn't find the words.

"You wanted to be a good friend," Adam said for her.

"I just wanted her to be happy; I've never seen her unhappy and I wouldn't want to. She's like this wonderful, perfect happy day and I love her so much." Kate's eyes filled with tears. She couldn't help it and it embarrassed her. "She's more like my sister. We know everything about each other, we do everything together, we go everywhere together," she tried to explain.

"Not everything," Adam said quietly.

"She knows about Loraine," Kate said.

"No, not that," he said.

Kate's teary eyes dried as confusion crossed her face.

"You said you've always liked me, she obviously doesn't know that," he said. Leave it to Adam to pay attention to the details.

"Actually, she does. She just doesn't remember it," Kate said, looking out the passenger window.

She sighed loudly as she turned to him. When she saw the confused look on his face she explained.

"I've had a...crush on you for a long time, and I told her and Cora a long time ago. Cora remembers it, but Abby does not, it was a long time ago," she said, trying to rationalize Abby's memory lapse.

Adam was silent, looking down at his hands which had fallen into his lap from the steering wheel. The engine was running, the heat was on and the minutes were passing.

Kate laid her head on the back of the seat and turned her body to Adam. Then, with her heart beginning to race, she scooted a little closer to him.

He looked at her and smiled, so she scooted closer and to her delight he put one hand on her hip and one between her head and the seat. He pulled her to him, so close she was warmed immediately. Her head found a nice spot just below his chin and he laid his cheek on the top of her head with his arm draped down her back.

Her neck cradled inside of her sweatshirt and her hand found his leg. She could feel him smelling her hair and she smiled. This moment was perfect and now she knew for certain that this was too good to let go of. This was what she longed for, even more than being captain of the cheerleading team. This time she would not take the back seat. Warmth filled every part of her body and she could feel her heart swell. Her body relaxed and a small sigh escaped her lips.

She looked up at him to ask him what he thought she should do about Abby, but when her face lifted to his, her lips were met with his. She felt them press against hers and instinctively her eyes closed. The kiss was sudden so Kate had no time to lose her breath. His tongue pressed against her lip so she opened her mouth slightly, letting him in. She lost herself in the sensuality, feeling his fingers brush against her cheek like she had always imagined, feeling the softness of his lips. It was the perfect kiss. He pulled away from her and when she opened her eyes he was smiling down at her. Neither of them said anything. She nuzzled her face closer to his and found the nook beneath his chin again.

They sat together for almost a half hour before Adam realized he was running low on gas.

"We better go," he said, lifting his arm from her and sitting up straight. Sleepily, she pulled herself into sitting position. She was pushing herself back into the passenger seat when Adam put his arm across her lap and pulled her back to him.

"Don't go anywhere," he said. He had pulled her as close to him as he could get her and then put the truck into gear.

They backed out of the parking spot and turned out into the road. Kate laid her head on his shoulder for the rest of the ride. Some twenty minutes later they were at Celia's apartment.

"You have a key, right?" He asked.

Kate remembered Celia's high voice telling her there was a spare key on the counter. She also remembered she didn't pick up before they left.

Kate puffed out her cheeks.

"Wellllll," Kate began. And then Adam's phone rang.

The sound was turned so high on his phone that Kate could hear Arthur on the other end.

"Hey, where are you guys?" Arthur asked.

"We had to get something eat, we were starving," Adam told him.

"Well, where are you now?" He asked.

"We're back, we went to Moe's," Adam said.

"Oooooooh," Arthur said. Obviously he knew it was pretty far from town.

"We're at Celia's apartment, but we don't have a key."

"OK, I'll be there in like five minutes, I'm down the road."

"Alright," Adam said, and then he clicked the phone off and put it in his pocket.

"He's on his way here," Adam said to Kate.

Kate cleared her throat and slid away from Adam slightly. She felt awkward about letting Arthur see her so close to Adam.

Adam must have been thinking the same because he didn't pull her back to him this time.

They sat in silence until they saw Arthur pull into the driveway.

"Why didn't you guys just go in?" Arthur said with a smile as they got out of their vehicles.

"No key, remember?" Adam said.

"Celia's home, you know. She keeps the lights off when she's not using them, it saves on the electric bill. She must be in the bathroom upstairs," he said as he looked at the dark apartment.

Sure enough, the door was unlocked and Arthur led them inside. Kate wanted so bad to follow close enough behind Adam as to feel his warmth, but she wasn't sure how she should act around Arthur. Upstairs Kate could hear a shower running.

Arthur plopped down in the middle of the couch and turned the television on. He thumbed through the channels as Kate sat in an overstuffed chair and Adam sat across the room on an ottoman.

"So how'd the research go?" He asked them.

"Hey Arthur," Adam said with a huff.

"Yeah?" Arthur said, eyes glued to ESPN.

"Kate's not working on a report," he started. Arthur continued to watch the screen.

"Kate's trying to find who murdered her sister," Adam let out.

It got Arthur's attention, which was Adam's intention. Arthur turned sharply to Adam with wide eyes.

"Actually, she disappeared," Kate said shyly. "We don't know if she was murdered."

Arthur turned to her. Confusion looked the same on his face as it had on Adam's. She could tell their resemblance very well.

"Since when do you have a sister?" He asked and then added, "I'm sorry, that sounded a little harsh, but, what I mean is, I don't remember you having a sister."

Kate smiled weakly at his apology, she was slightly embarrassed.

"Well, actually, she disappeared before I was even born," Kate explained. Kate went on to tell about the mysterious disappearance and the location.

"But don't tell anyone, I mean, Kate kind of wants to keep it a secret," Adam said.

Arthur took a deep breath in as the situation began to settle with him.

"Fair enough," he said, nodding. He didn't seem interested in knowing the reason for it being a secret.

They heard the bathroom door open on the floor above them and Arthur peered up the staircase.

"Love?" He yelled up to her.

"Yes, dear, I'm here. Where are your brother and his friend?" She called down.

"They're here. Hurry down," he said.

"Even from Celia," Adam whispered immediately. Kate hadn't thought about having to ask Arthur to keep it from his girlfriend. But perhaps it was best, at least for now.

Arthur nodded an 'OK'.

"We're going tomorrow to talk to old neighbors. Do you want to go?" Adam whispered.

"Yeah, I'll go. Celia has class all day anyway," he said.

"Class on a Saturday?" Kate asked. Maybe college wasn't as spectacular as she had imagined it.

"Yeah, it's an all-day course they have every Saturday for six weeks. Celia only has classes Thursday, Friday and Saturday because she works in the Research Department Monday through Wednesday."

On second thought, maybe college *was* spectacular. People not only got to choose what classes they took, but also got to choose what time and day they wanted to take them. Kate was running her potential schedules through her head when Celia came down the stairs. She was wearing cotton pajama pants, a thin white t-shirt and slippers. Her mousy hair was still a bit wet and fell flat on her shoulders. She skipped the last step, fluted past Kate and jumped on the couch beside Arthur, sitting on her legs. She gripped his chin in her fingers, turning it to her and planted a loud kiss on his cheek. He smiled at her and kissed her lips quickly, but lightly and then patted the side of her legs.

"How was class?" Kate asked.

Celia let out a long sigh and said, "oooh my gosh. It was so boring. It's an intro to physics class that I have to take before I can take physics and quantum physics. But I had a physics class in high school so it's all a repeat to me."

"You had physics in high school?" Kate asked. Their high school didn't have a physics class. They had pre-calculus and that was as advanced as it got.

"Celia went to private school, ivy league. She's a little rich girl," Arthur teased.

Celia giggled and said, "Whatever, Arthur."

That explained the expensive items in the apartment.

"So are you guys coming to Queens next year?" She asked, looking from Adam to Kate. Kate and her mother had visited college campuses around West Virginia. They had also visited the Student Financial Aid departments and that's when Kate learned the expense of an education. She had decided very early on that she would take classes at the Community College that was twenty minutes from town, only a thirty-minute drive from her house.

"Adam has a different idea," Arthur answered. Kate realized she didn't know what Adam had planned for his life after high school.

"I don't think I'm going to go," Adam said.

Two thoughts crossed her mind: *Good, you'll be near me* and *But you got to go to college.* Kate sat quietly. She decided saying anything at this moment might be bad.

"What about you, Kate?" Arthur asked.

"Um, I think I'll do the first two years at Change Modei Community College. I'll transfer after to finish a bachelor's," she said.

Celia looked at the floor and Adam followed suit.

"Are you guys hungry?" Celia asked, changing the subject.

"We just ate," Kate said at the same time Adam was saying, "No, we had Moe's."

"Well, I didn't have anything and I'm hungry," she said, getting up.

"Want soup, Arthur?" She asked as she made her way into the kitchen.

"Na, I had something at Jay's," he said.

"Chips and refried bean dip, I bet," she said through the bar.

"Maaaaybe," Arthur responded, smiling as if he were caught doing something he wasn't supposed to be doing.

"You're going to get fat eating that junk, dear," she said.

Arthur didn't say anything, he just smiled.

"So what did you guys do all day?" She asked.

Everyone was quiet until Arthur was able to say, "we watched football at Jay's."

The answer seemed to work well. Celia was obviously not OK with the silence and so she asked, "well, who won?"

"The Raiders," Arthur answered, and then silence again.

Adam and Arthur began talking about a motorcycle their father had recently bought. Celia either didn't eat much soup, or ate it very quickly because it wasn't too much longer that she appeared in the room again.

"I should probably show you where you'll be sleeping. My roommate Jessica has gone home for the weekend and she said it would be fine for you to sleep in her bed. I put fresh sheets, blankets and pillowcases on," she said as she began to walk up the stairs.

Kate jumped up and followed her. When they got to the top landing Celia stopped and then motioned Kate closer to her.

Celia whispered, "Listen, Jessica is a little...freaky." She pulled Kate into the room and turned the light on.

"She's really into sex. A lot of sex, all the time, freaky sex," Celia said. "I flipped the mattress, she's a clean person, just...well, you know. If you're still uncomfortable sleeping on it, I have two large bean bags that make a surprisingly comfortable bed. Honest. I sleep in them all the time."

Kate thought for a moment. The girl who stayed in this room was having sex, actually doing it, going all the way. She realized the girl must have been only a few years older than her. Kate knew of some girls at school who had done it, but she'd never really had a boyfriend. She had kissed boys, even let one go up her shirt at a party once on a dare. But this girl whose room she was about to borrow was really doing it. She wondered if Arthur and Celia...and she stopped. She didn't really want to think about it. Then she wondered if Adam had...

"Uh, I'll take the bed," she said, forcing her thoughts away. She felt certain that flipping a mattress would make it OK.

"Alright then," Celia said and walked out and back down the stairs, leaving Kate to herself.

Although it was odd for Celia to just leave her there, Kate was distracted by mystery girl's space. There were posters of jazz bands and hot guys dressed in grunge style clothing. The girl's bed was a four poster with lace curtains tied to the posts. At the foot of the bed was an old wooden chest. On one wall was a small desk with a large Macintosh screen and a metal tower beneath. Adjacent were a set of double doors, what Kate assumed was the closet. On the opposite wall was a window, Kate rushed over to see what was out back.

Halfway there she heard Celia panting into the room. Turning, she saw Celia lugging in Kate's bag.

"Oh, I forgot about that, let me take it," Kate said rushing over. She was embarrassed that Celia had remembered to get it before she had.

"Oh, it's no problem," Celia said.

"Celia, we're leaving!" They heard from downstairs. It was Arthur.

Celia and Kate made their way back downstairs. Celia tippy-toed to give Arthur a peck on the lips. Kate looked at her shoes and Adam looked away, toward the door. Arthur wrapped his arm around

Celia as they kissed and then he opened the door. Adam waved to Kate before slipping out the door, Kate smiled.

When the door closed Celia locked it. She turned to Kate and said, "whoa…what was that?"

Kate looked at her, confused.

"That smile," she said, with a big smile of her own. Celia had picked up on the awkward goodbye.

Kate just shrugged.

"Sooo…what's between you and Adam?" She asked.

"Nothing," Kate lied, turning to walk up the stairs.

"Oh, whatever," Celia said, smiling, as she followed Kate up.

"He's seeing my best friend," Kate said.

"Yeah?" Celia asked.

When Kate reached the landing she quickly scooted into the bedroom.

"Do you like him though?" She asked, then added, "you can tell me." This was as if saying, 'you can trust me,' but Kate had been around that circle before one too many times. When girls at school had said 'you can tell me', it meant that you could tell them so they could tell everyone else. She didn't know if she could trust Celia at all.

"Of course not," Kate said, shutting the door. She knew it was rude, but she was caught off guard. How could this girl that she just met tune into her feelings for Adam? It couldn't be *that* obvious. Could it? Apparently so.

Kate listened for Celia's footsteps, but she must have been a light walker because she couldn't hear anything. After a moment, when she was sure Celia had gone, Kate opened the door just enough to be able to see out onto the landing. Across the way she saw Celia's door was closed. A pretty pink and purple sign on the door read, "Cuties Only". She could hear the low sound of music coming from Celia's door. She was sorry she had shut her out, but she wasn't sure what was between her and Adam. She just knew she wasn't ready to talk about it.

CHAPTER SEVEN

She was in the woods and the sun had gone down long ago. Her heart raced and she could see her breath in the night air.

Something to her left stepped on a stick and it broke. Quickly she turned to face the noise, fearful. Her mind reeled for ways to get out of the way and to get away from the thing. To her right there was another noise. As soon as she jerked her head to look in that direction, a soft voice whispered in left ear, "near the pond." Turning quickly to the left, the voice seemed to fade away into the night like a light fog. Off in the distance straight ahead she heard footsteps more clearly, breaking leaves and branches as they came toward her. Instead of hiding she tried to narrow her focus to see what was coming. Then she saw a boot, then another and a pair of legs coming toward her. They were thick, heavy legs, very muscular and they definitely belonged to a man. A full figure came into her view. It was a tall man wearing light brown Carhartt overalls and steel-toed boots. He carried a walking stick and walked like he was strong. His body was built, save for a large belly.

Kate woke up with a start. She had been lying in the fetal position, but the upper half of her body was elevated by many fluffed pillows. Her elbow was crooked and her cheek lay on her knuckles. She had fallen asleep sitting up halfway and woken up in the same position. Looking out the window she could see it was still dark outside. She grabbed her phone from the bedside table and saw that it was only 4:00 AM.

The feeling the dream left her with disappeared rather quickly as her mind wandered back to Adam. She wondered if he was sleeping. She wondered if he snored. *I can't let him continue to distract me*, she thought as she realized nearly all her thoughts were of him now instead of finding what happened to Loraine.

Kate got out of bed and sat at the computer desk. She turned on the desk lamp and snatched up a piece of computer paper and a pen from the pencil holder. She wanted to record what she had seen in her dream. Somehow she recognized that it would have something to do with Loraine. As she scrawled down every detail she could remember, she thought about previous dreams she had. She thought back to the dream she had where she and Abby were playing hide-go-seek in the cemetery. Instantly that feeling of having lost her friend washed over her and hurt filled her heart. It was the same way she had felt in the truck when she was telling Adam how much Abby meant to her. It was so thick she had to stop writing and let the tears come. It seemed absurd to be crying over nothing, but the feeling would not go away and she was feeling bad for having kissed Adam.

Finally Kate stood up and stretched. She went downstairs to get a glass of water, hoping the feeling would leave. When she reached the bottom of the stairs she felt around on the wall for the light switch. The room flooded with light as she flipped the nub and everything was still. The TV was dark, the room was empty. This did not help Kate's mood. She turned on the lights in the kitchen as well and stood listening to the sound of the refrigerator for a long minute. The cemetery dream replayed in her head and she couldn't find the strength to stop it.

Just as the large man appeared to tell her Abby was dead, she forced herself to move. Kate opened the fridge and the bright light seemed to smooth the feeling over. She pulled out a Brita container and set it on the counter. Leaving the fridge open, she searched through the cabinets to find a small glass. She wished the sun would hurry up and rise, the darkness of the night was not helping to rid her of the feelings. She gulped down the whole glass of water, threw the glass in the sink and put the Brita container back in the fridge. Closing the fridge, she turned around and realized there was someone else in the room, standing right in front of her.

Her heart lurched forward as flashes of the heavy, booted man tore through her mind. But quickly she recognized it was Celia, but not before she let out a startled sound.

"I'm sorry, I didn't mean to frighten you," Celia said, touching Kate's elbow.

"I just wanted to tell you that I'm sorry for prying earlier," she said as Kate's breaths began to slow.

"No," Kate said. "*I'm* sorry. I didn't mean to be so terse." Kate was impressed with herself for using such a collegiate word…and using it correctly. She hoped it impressed Celia as well.

"I just…" Kate sat down in a chair nearby.

"It's OK," Celia said. "I understand. I shouldn't have been so nosy."

"No, it wasn't that," Kate said. She opened her mouth to tell Celia more, but hesitated. She looked up at Celia, trying to read her face for some hint of anything that would tell Kate she could trust Celia. Kate decided to make a leap.

"I do like Adam. And he likes me, but…my friend Abby. She's kind of seeing him, they're together," she tried to explain.

"Does your friend know you're with him? Right now, I mean."

"No. That's what makes it so horrible. But it wasn't like that when we left. I came here--" and Kate stopped. How would she explain the next part?

"You came here and?" Celia pressed.

Kate's mind reeled trying desperately to come up with something to tell Celia.

"I came to see the campus. My mother went to Queens University, I thought it would be good to just see it," Kate lied. It was very weak, but she hoped it would be good enough for Celia.

Kate noticed Celia's shoulders drop. She could tell Celia knew she was lying. But Kate wasn't going to tell her about Loraine. Even though Celia probably didn't know anyone at all back home in West Virginia, she still did not feel comfortable telling her this private piece of her. She wasn't sure why, but she didn't quite fully trust Celia, but she wanted to trust her.

"We should probably go back to bed," Kate said.

"Yeah," Celia said with a disappointed look on her face. Kate could tell she wanted to hear more, but she didn't want to part with any more information.

When Kate got back to her room she looked at her phone again. She had a text. She hadn't noticed it before when she looked at the time.

'Are you awake?' It said. It was from Adam.

Kate text back, "I am now." She looked at the time the text had been sent and saw that it had arrived at 2:09 am. Surely he would be asleep now. But to her surprise, within seconds of putting the phone back on the stand, it lit up. This time the text read, 'what are you doing up?' So Kate responded, 'what are *you* doing up?'

'Reading,' was his response.

'Reading what?' She asked.

'Police reports' was the response.

'Police reports?' She asked.

'Yeah. They r avail online,' he texted.

'What r u lookn 4?' She texted.

'Nothing n particlr,' he responded. Kate smiled at this new bit of knowledge. Adam liked to read police reports at four in the morning.

'Go 2 sleep,' she texted.

'Can't,' he replied.

'Y?' She asked.

'Don't sleep well,' he texted. When she didn't respond for a few moments he texted back, 'insominia I guess…wat r u doin?'

'Had a bad dream,' she answered. Her breath caught at his next text.

'Wish I had been there to hold you.' Her smile was instant and spread from ear to ear.

'Me too' she typed. She stared at the words before she sent them. Did she really want to do this to Abby? She held the phone in her hand. She thought about Adam and his warm hands caressing her face, her neck and an exposed, bare shoulder. She let her mind wander to a place where Adam's bare chest looked dark against clean, white, cotton sheets and he held onto her when she awoke frightened. Without letting herself think about Abby she hit the send button. As soon as she did, an unfamiliar boulder replaced her gut. It was heavy inside her.

'Don't cry' was the text back. How could he know?! She found it amusing and a smile travelled across her face again.

'I'm not' she texted. Technically it was true, she wasn't crying. But she had been on the verge of it.

Kate began to feel tired and wondered if she'd be able to fall back to sleep. As the moments passed she became sleepier and sleepier. She was fading out when she noticed her phone light up.

'Did I lose u?' He asked.

'No' she typed. She couldn't find the energy to type more. She hit send.

'Falling asleep?' The next one asked. Again and again she was amazed at how well he was able to read her, even when they were nowhere near each other.

'Yes,' she sent.

'Goodnight. Sweet dreams,' he texted back.

She smiled at the last part and drifted off to sleep.

Around 8:00 a.m. the next morning Kate awoke. As she lifted her head up, a string of drool connected her to the pillow. *Gross*, she thought. Kate wiped the spit from her cheek and mouth and sat up. The room might have been more inviting if more light was let in, but the crimson red, thick curtains blocked the majority of it out. She made her way to the window and pulled the curtains back. Out the window she saw small concrete patios for each of the townhouses. Beyond them was a large grassy field. Just a distance away Kate could see volleyball nets. *I can't wait to live on my own*, she thought.

She took the extra clothes from her bag and went to the bathroom for a shower, passing Celia's shut door. Afterward she blow dried her hair and curled the ends with what she hoped was Celia's curling iron. She came out of the bathroom dressed and ready to get started. She noticed Celia's door was wide open.

Looking into the room Kate could see a very clean, organized room. Even though it was day, the lights were on and Kate could tell the white light bulbs had been replaced with purple ones. They made the room appear to be a light purple. *Neat idea*, she thought. But Celia was not there. She must have left for class while Kate was in the shower.

She sat on the side of the bed and typed in her text. 'What time can we leave?' It was almost nine in the morning, surely they would be awake. She hit send. Minutes passed and there was no response so she went downstairs to find something to eat. The cabinets were bare, no cereal, no oatmeal, no bread. There was no milk or juice in the fridge. The realities of college living began to sink in.

Kate sat in one of the two chairs at the table and listened as her stomach growled. Her phone lit up and before she checked the message she put it on vibrate and ring. The message read 'We'll b thr n 10 mins'.

Kate sat on the couch and waited. Almost a half hour later she heard a car pull up in the driveway. It was Arthur and Adam.

She slid into her jacket as she was closing the door. This time she didn't forget the key and locked it from the outside. Adam was driving; Arthur had gotten into the backseat so Kate slid into the passenger side front seat.

"So where do we start?" Adam asked.

"I guess the neighborhood. The house is at 234 Elm. Do you know that area, Arthur?"

"No, that's a suburban area," he said. Kate had never known the house. The cousin was on her father's side of the family.

Adam programmed the address into the GPS and they set off. When they reached the residential area Kate realized the neighborhood was in disarray. Many houses were dilapidated with trash and large auto parts in their yards. She guessed that twenty years ago the neighborhood hadn't looked like it did now. She imagined the houses a brighter white with green lawns and happy children playing outside.

Adam pulled the car over to the curb.

"There it is," he said, pointing across the street to a brick house. It was a single level home that at one time must have been very nice. A small porch with a few steps still existed and a very old Buick sat in the driveway.

There it is, Kate thought. It was the porch her sister had disappeared from. One minute she was sitting there and the next minute she was not. She tried to picture her sister sitting on the steps in the hot summer sun.

Adam opened his door to get out.

"No, I'll go," Kate said. She wanted to do it alone. Perhaps the family had moved away a long time ago. Perhaps they still lived in the house. She didn't know, but she would find out.

Kate jogged across the road and onto the sidewalk and then made her way across the brown grass to the steps. Hesitating, she rapped on the door. Inside she heard something stir, but heard no footsteps coming to the door. She knocked again, and again she heard something, but no one came to the door.

"Hello!" She called.

Finally she heard someone making their way to the door.

The door opened only slightly, just a sliver.

"What do you want?" She heard.

"Um, I just wanted to ask you something. How long have you lived here?" Kate asked shyly. She hadn't thought about what she would say to anyone who answered the door.

"Who are you?" The female voice demanded.

"My name is Kate Cooper. I'm--" Kate thought that the real story might be a little strange to the old woman, and she found herself trying to come up with another lie. *Boy all this lying I've done lately is annoying*, Kate thought.

"I used to live here and I'm trying to find an old stuffed animal I had. When you moved here, were there any bags or things left behind?" *I am definitely not a good liar*, she thought.

"No, now go away," The voice said and she closed the door.

"Please," Kate begged through the door. "I just…fine. My sister disappeared from this neighborhood a long time ago. I'm just trying to see if I can find something that would help us figure out what happened to her.

"Are you a cop?" The voice asked.

"No. No, I'm a student," Kate said. The house was silent again. Seconds seemed like minutes and Kate was ready to give up, but then she had an idea.

"Her cousins lived here in 1993, she was fourteen. She came to see them, but her cousin was babysitting, so she decided to wait on the porch until her aunt and uncle came home. That was the last time anyone saw her. She disappeared from this porch. Please, tell me how long you've lived here."

But nothing on the other side stirred until the door opened slightly again.

"I remember that," the voice said from the other side. "I never knew it was this house."

"Do you know who lived her before you? Do you remember the name of the people you bought the house from?" Kate asked.

"Daphne and Roger Lennels," she said. "I bought the house in 1996."

"Do you know where they moved to?" Kate asked.

"Florida, I do believe. Somewhere near a beach, I remember." Then suddenly the woman became aggravated. "Oh hell, just go look at the deed information, it's public you know!" And she slammed the door. Kate knew this was all the information she was going to get, so she crossed the street and got back in the car, defeated.

"Nothing?" Adam asked.

Kate replayed the event and told them what the old woman had told her, word for word.

"Now there's an idea," Arthur said. "Let's go to the Court House. We can look at the deeds to the properties and see all the previous owners."

"They keep that information?" Adam asked.

"Yeah, of course. That's how they know who to tax," Arthur said with a smile.

"Awesome," Kate said.

Adam put the car into gear and as he pulled onto the road he said, "I hope they're open on a Saturday."

"Oh they are," Arthur said. "But only until noon."

"How do you know?" Adam asked.

"I'm taking a property law class," he said.

Ten minutes later they were parking at the large County Courthouse. Inside Arthur took them right to the records room where they signed in. It didn't take Arthur long to find the parcels of property they were interested in. Then all they had to do was look for the year 1993.

The records rooms were dark and smelled like old book glue, a smell Kate loved. Large, old ledger books and record books were on hundreds of shelves that went on forever. Every four or five shelves there was a small gap where there was a work table. Arthur had grabbed numerous books and handed some to Kate and some to Arthur as they made their way to a work table some thirty shelves into the room. Kate was surrounded by books and shelves.

The book that Arthur had opened had handwritten names in it. They were scrawled in old-hand cursive writing and none of them could read the names properly. When they got to recent years, the writing became legible. Finally Arthur turned the page and they all saw a copy of a deed that had May 12, 1996 as a sell date.

Arthur bent forward over the pages to read more clearly because the writing had faded.

"Daphne and Roger Lennels to…" Arthur flipped the page and finished, "Mason McGregor."

"So the name is right," Kate said.

"Let's see who Daphne and Roger bought it from," Adam said, flipping the pages backward.

"Hmm, looks like we're looking for Daphne and Roger. They bought it from the Townsends in 1985."

"Let's find out who owned the house across the street," Kate said.

Arthur showed Kate and Adam how to find the deeds they needed and within an hour and a half they had the names of all the individuals who owned the houses on the whole street and half of the next one over.

"Do you think it's enough?" Adam asked.

"How about I stay here. That way I can get some of my work done for class and you guys can…" Arthur hesitated and then finished, "can start interviewing people."

Kate noticed Arthur's hesitation and wondered if Adam had told Arthur about their kiss. She almost wanted to be angry, but how could she? Arthur was his brother, his confidant and for some reason, it really didn't bother her knowing Arthur knew their secret. As she was closing the books she'd had opened she wondered how things would be when they got back home. Would it go back to normal? Would Abby and Adam still be together making Kate even more miserable than before? Would Adam tell Abby and break her heart? Her stomach lurched at the thought and the terrible stone appeared again.

Adam appeared beside her and touched her hand. She felt his fingertips brush her lower back lightly.

"Let's go," he whispered, leaning in close to her ear. She found it very comforting and closed the last book. As they walked out she dropped it on the cart. She would hate to be the person whose job it was to put all the large books back on the shelves.

As soon as they got out into the cold air and away from Arthur, Adam laced his fingers into hers.

"Does Arthur know?" Kate asked him.

"Sort of," Adam answered.

"Sort of?" Kate asked.

"Well, you see--" he said as he shifted his body. After a moment he continued. "I've liked you for a while, Arthur's always known that. I had already told him about the situation with Abby…before."

Kate understood, which reinforced that it was really happening. She had fallen for Adam. But Abby was going to get hurt. Even though her stomach was growling, it was a mess.

"I think Abby will understand," he said. "She should care about your happiness as much as you care about hers. Maybe we could try to explain it to her."

But Kate didn't want to think about it. She wanted to forget all about Abby and concentrate on finding what happened to her sister…and to concentrate on Adam.

They spent the afternoon knocking on the doors of the houses in the neighborhood, asking for the owners by name. Sometimes the people who lived in the homes weren't the people who owned the property. Sometimes the people were supportive, sometimes they were aggravated. Some were helpful, some were not. One house on the corner was on property belonging to a David Shredder, who had bought his house in 1998 from Lynn and Reginald Cartwright. Reginald had passed away and Lynn now lived at an assisted living facility an hour away but David had always owned the next lot over. It had been handed down from his grandfather who had gotten it from his grandfather. In 1993 David lived in a mobile home on the property. He had been the same age as her sister and had gone to school with her.

"Was there anyone in town that everyone made fun of and picked on at the time? Someone that maybe bullies really went for?" Adam asked, remembering his aunt's reading for Kate.

"Not that I remember, we all got along well here. We played hide-go-seek through the neighborhood. All the kids would get together; we'd play until the sun went down. Loraine played with us a number of times, nearly always. I remember when she disappeared. My mom wouldn't let me go anywhere without someone with me for a long time after that," the man said in reverie.

"If you would have suspected someone, who would it have been?" Kate asked.

David looked to the ceiling and bunched his lips up, thinking. "You know I had thought about that back then. We all had our theories. Some of us thought it was a stranger, an out-of-towner. Some of us thought it was old Mr. Firet because there was a rumor he liked to fondle little girls, but me, I was never really able to pick someone out. It was one of those things, you know? Just one of them things that you think won't ever happen to you or your family or loved ones or friends. It was just what it was. After a while I think everyone gave up on speculatin'."

"Do you remember where you were when you heard about Loraine missing?" Adam asked.

"Yeah, I was down at the diner. My buddies Greg and Larry and I had gone in for a soda. It was horrible hot out that day. You could have fried an egg on the blacktop, it was so hot," then David chuckled and said, "But I guess that's another story."

"We were sitting at the bar top drinkin' sodas and a woman comes in all in a tizzy. It was Mrs. Bupis, I recognized her from church. Her face was tear stained and her lips were swollen. She came to the counter and stood closest to me. She whispered to the waitress who called for the owner of the diner. He came out with his chef apron on and nearly everyone in the place heard Mrs. Bupis' tear-filled story. Loraine Cooper was missing since yesterday, stolen right off the front porch of the Lennels' place."

"That afternoon nearly the whole neighborhood had gotten together and combed the streets looking for her. The police said she must have run away, but I think we all knew better. Loraine wasn't no trouble-maker, she was a straight A student, always did perfect in anythin', sort of a do-gooder if you ask me. She was a cute girl though; cute enough people thought it was some nutter that ran off with her to do dirty things to her. We all assumed as much anyways."

Now David looked up at Kate.

"I'm sorry. Does it bother you when I say those things? I didn't think, I'm real sorry," he began apologizing.

"Oh, no, that's fine. Really. I never knew her. This was all before I was even born," she explained.

"How old are you?" He asked.

"Seventeen," she answered. David just nodded his head.

"I'm sorry I can't help you, but if you ever want me to share some memories I had of Loraine, you can call me. I got family what all that's left is someone else's memories, so I know how it is," he said.

"I'll do that," she said standing up to leave.

"Let me get you my number," he said, going into the kitchen. He returned a few moments later and wrote his number down on a small piece of paper.

He handed it to her and said, "Day or night, long as it's not night." Then he laughed heartily at his own joke.

Adam shook David's hand and said goodbye as they headed out the door. David stood in the doorway as they walked toward the truck and called to them, "You kids stay safe! And good luck!"

This was the first place where they were able to walk away with something more than they had. They now had an idea of how the neighborhood was when Loraine lived there. It seemed to be a tight-knit area, the kind of place where everyone knew everyone else. They got the impression the town was comprised of caring families and church-goers. But the next stop would give them an entirely different idea.

The next two houses on the block were for sale and no one was home at the third house. Across the street, on the opposite corner from David's current lot, stood another brick house that was very similar to the Lennel's house.

Adam knocked hard on the door and immediately on the other side they heard someone responding. The steps were slow. Eventually the door opened slightly and they could see a tall, dark-skinned woman with hair that had turned gray ages ago. She wore a long, flowery dress and gripped tightly to a light-colored cane that had a rubber bottom. The woman didn't look at them; she looked past them and squinted her eyes tight.

"Hello?" She called.

Adam realized it before Kate. The woman was blind.

"Oh, we're right here, Ms. Langley," Adam said sweetly.

"Who are you?" She asked, staring into the air.

"I'm Adam and this is Kate--" he began, but was quickly interrupted.

"I don't want to buy anything today, but maybe come back tomorrow," she said and started to close the door.

Kate quickly pressed her hand again the door and said, "we're not here to sell anything Ms. Langley."

"We wanted to ask you about a girl who disappeared in this neighborhood in 1993," Adam finished.

"A girls gone missin'?" She asked.

"No, not now," Kate said. "It was in 1993. She disappeared in 1993."

"Hon, you got to speak up, I'm blind as a bat and nearly deaf."

Kate repeated herself, louder the second time.

"Would you maybe sit with us on your porch so we can talk about it?" Adam asked.

The porch was the only thing different about the house from the Lennels' house. The porch stretched the length of the front of the house and had a very nice porch swing and thick, white, sturdy, wood railing.

"Nineteen ninety-three," the woman repeated, and began nodding her head. "That was the same year my daughter graduated college." The woman smiled big. She was obviously super proud of her daughter for the accomplishment. Ms. Langley brought her cane in front of her and leaned heavily on it.

"That was the year my son went to prison," she continued. "So strange how two kids from the same parents could turn out such opposites of each other."

"Do you remember a girl named Loraine who lived in this neighborhood?" Kate asked, interrupting.

"Loraine…no, no I don't think I do, but my memories aren't so good anymore," she said.

"They had a search party for her. They combed the whole town," Adam said, trying to get her to remember anything.

"Nope, I don't remember anything like that. This neighborhood couldn't come together for anything, too many people hatin' other people for no good reasons. 'Oh your dogs on my property, so I shot it' or 'your son tried lookin' up my girl's skirt so I beat him' things like that all the time. Once some retarded boy got hisself stuck in a tree and not a single person tried to help him down. They all listened to him wail and cry in that tree for nearly the whole night 'fore someone called the po-leese. You'd think his mama would be concerned for her retarded boy, but noooo, not that hot to trot trash. No, no, she whipped that boy all the way home I would bet, no mercy. People round here don't care much 'bout each other. Never did, neither."

"Are you sure you don't remember? It was all over the news," Adam asked, but the old woman stood there just shaking her head.

Kate wanted to write down her number to give to the woman, in case she remembered something later. Her face flushed as she caught herself before asking the question. The blind woman wouldn't be able to read the numbers.

"If I can tell you my number, could you be able to remember it? That way you can call me if you do happen to remember something." Kate said.

"You can tell me it, I use a label maker to make braille, you kids stay right here and let me get it," she said, turning around slowly and heading back inside, leaving the door wide open.

"Ingenuity," Adam said.

The woman reappeared and said, "OK, go slowly now." Kate gave the woman her cell phone number and wondered why the woman didn't have any of the logical tools that many blind individuals had today.

By this time Kate's stomach was so empty that her head was beginning to hurt. She looked at her phone. It was almost noon.

"I'm going to faint if I don't get something to eat," she told Adam.

"There's a convenience store around the block," he said. "It'd be quickest."

They walked around the block and went inside the store. There they bought soup and Adam got a deli sandwich. When they were finished Kate sat back in the booth and sighed loudly. She felt like they were getting nowhere.

Adam opened his mouth to say something when Kate's phone rang. She dug it out of her pocket and looked at the number that was calling. She didn't recognize it, but answered it anyway.

"Hello?" She said.

"Hi. This is Johnathan Morrow, I'm looking for Adam," she heard. Her eyes grew large as she looked over to Adam who was swallowing big gulp of turkey sandwich.

"This is Kate, Adam was calling for me," Kate sat up straight. "We were wondering if you'd be able to meet with us sometime today?"

"Well, unfortunately I'm out of town for the next month, so I doubt that'd be possible unless you're in Colorado," he said.

"Um, no," she said into the phone, disappointed. "We wanted to talk to you about a case you had in 1993. It was the disappearance of Loraine Cooper."

"That doesn't ring a bell and all my case files and notes are locked up there in Charlotte. I can't get to them so there's very little I can tell you at the moment. What would you like to know?"

Kate felt hopeless. "We just wanted to know everything and anything you could tell us."

"And what is this for?" The retired detective asked.

"She's my sister," Kate said. "Well, she was my sister. She disappeared before I was born."

"I see," he said. "I'm sorry I can't help you. But I would suggest giving the police station a call and asking them to put it in the Cold Case bin for re-review. That usually speeds things up. Don't go looking for anything on your own. Even though you might not think so, it could be a very dangerous situation that should be handled by professionals, so contact Cold Case and let them do their job."

"Thank you for your help," Kate said into the phone. She heard Detective Morrow say goodbye and he hung up.

"He said he's in Colorado, doesn't have access to his files. He wants us to contact the cold case people to restart the search," she told Adam.

"You know, that might be a good idea. We'll get something stirred up again, to get real investigators to do it properly," he said. But honestly he didn't really want that. He wanted the adventure. He wanted something to share with Kate; the opportunity to be closer to her.

Kate only stared into her soup. Adam's phone rang. She imagined it was Arthur because Adam was giving a run-down of their day. After a few 'uh-huhs' and 'alrights', Adam clicked the phone.

"Arthur's ready to go. They must have kicked him out when they closed," Adam said with a smile.

That was it. That was all there was. She had come to NC, she had investigated, she had found information, but it wasn't enough. Loraine was still mysteriously disappeared. She was surely defeated now and she had only searched and researched for less than forty-eight hours.

As always, Adam knew what she was feeling.

"Don't give up yet. An answer might lie behind the next door," he said. But she was not hopeful. She wanted to quit and she expected Adam had grown tired of asking the same questions over and over again to a different face each time. They walked the block and half back to Arthur's car and got inside. It was good to feel the heat, even though it wasn't terribly cold out that day.

"You know, if we don't get anywhere this weekend, we can come back next weekend," Adam suggested. Kate smiled. She would go anywhere with Adam, but perhaps it was time to give up on finding out what happened to her sister. What had made her think she could find anything anyway?

Adam put his hand on her knee and shook it lightly to comfort her. He started the vehicle and put it into gear. He pulled out of the parking lot and onto the road, headed north toward the county courthouse. When they arrived Arthur was waiting out front on the steps. Adam pulled up near the front and Arthur jumped in the back seat.

"I was able to get the names for half the properties on the next road," he reported.

Seeing how excited Arthur was about it all made Kate feel rejuvenated. She had help, like she wanted.

"Let's get organized," Kate said, turning to face Adam in the car and where Arthur could hear her clearly from the back seat.

"Some of the questions that got the most information from people that we used were 'do you remember Loraine' or any variation of remembering the event happening in the neighborhood. 'Did you know her or the family' and 'what were you doing when you found out she was missing' were questions that usually got people talking more. Also, you'll want to ask everyone if there was anyone in the neighborhood that the other kids picked on and made fun of," Kate said.

"Why's that?" Arthur asked. Kate had thought Adam would have told him about visiting their aunt. She looked toward Adam but Adam didn't say anything.

"Well, your aunt told us it might be useful to ask," she said.

"My aunt? I only got one aunt and...Aunt Nabhanya?" Arthur asked. "*Our* Aunt Nabhanya? Oh my gosh," he said, rolling his eyes.

"Look, Arthur," Adam began

"Listen, Kate. You can't take anything Nabhanya says seriously. She's just an old lady who wants attention. She can't really "see" anything." He told her.

"She told me about Loraine. No one in that whole town knew about Loraine," Kate countered.

"Arthur, you have to realize that what she…" Adam tried to break in.

"She probably knew the moment you moved into town, what do you think she does all day? She sits and reads about people, I mean really," Arthur went on, keeping Adam from speaking.

"There's no way she could have known about it," Kate threw in.

"I know you don't believe it, but--" Adam continued trying to break into the conversation.

"Think about it: a sleepy town with two new people moving in down the road? Of course she's going to research you, know you without knowing you, that's what she does," Arthur went on.

All the talking began rattling around in Kate's head.

"OK, stop, just stop," she said. Both Adam and Arthur stopped talking.

"Fine, it doesn't matter what she said, just ask the question. It isn't going to hurt anything to ask it," Kate said. She watched Arthur collapse back in the seat with a sigh, stuffing his hands into his jacket pockets. She wondered if he would ask the question or not.

"Please?" Kate asked, looking back at him.

"Alright," Arthur said, agitated. Kate had never seen Arthur come unglued before; she had never imagined it either. Even though he gave off the impression he was calm and collected all the time, she now realized that he really wasn't. She wondered what else would upset him like that. Apparently the subject of Nabhanya needed to be avoided or at least approached lightly.

"So let's split up the remaining houses," Adam said. "We have some left on Pear Street, and then there are the ones you got on Acorn Street. Why don't Kate and I take Pear Street and you can handle Acorn?"

"Maybe we should all go together," Kate suggested. She still didn't trust Arthur to ask about a kid that was picked on a lot. Arthur was quiet.

"OK, let's finish Pear Street then," Adam said.

They drove back south and parked on the street adjacent to Pear Street. They walked back to the house where they had left off. This house was a very nice house, made of stone and brick. The drive way was paved and the lawn was very well manicured. The outside of the house had been kept in good condition. Obviously, someone was still living there.

All three walked up to the door and Kate rang the bell. After a few moments, a tall, dark-skinned man opened the door. He looked like he might have been in his late twenties or early thirties. The man looked down at them as two toddler-aged kids screamed for his attention somewhere behind him. He didn't even say hello.

"Um, hi, we're wondering if you lived here in 1993?" Kate asked.

"Why?" The man asked as a toddler wrapped its arms and legs around the man's legs.

"My sister, Loraine, went missing from this neighborhood in 1993 and we wondered if you'd remember it," Kate explained.

"Missing girl in 1993. No, I don't remember anything like that," he said.

"Would your wife remember? Is she home?" Adam asked.

"She's working, but I don't think you need to come around here asking no questions like that without a police officer," he said.

"We're asking everyone in the neighborhood," Arthur tried.

"I'm just trying to find my sister," Kate said after.

The man peered out the door, down the street and then up the street the other way.

"Alright. I do remember it. I was young when it happened. But I don't know what would have happened to her. Maybe some family member ran off with her, that's what usually happens when kids go missin'," he said.

"Do you remember who she hung out with?" Adam asked.

"Naw, I didn't know her so well, she was a lot older than me," he said.

"Do you remember if there was any particular person in town who the kids all made fun of, might have picked on a lot?" Adam asked.

"Oh gees," the man laughed. "Everybody pretty much picked on everybody." The man became at ease and leaned his body against the door frame.

"We'd all be running around playing pranks on each other, trying to get a rise," he said.

"But was there any particular kid who got made fun of the most?" Kate asked.

"No one comes to my mind really," he said.

"Thanks for your time," Adam said, and they turned to walk away.

"Sorry I couldn't help you more," he said.

"Let me leave you my phone number. When your wife gets home, ask her if she remembers the disappearance and ask her if she knew of someone who was bullied more than the others. If she does, just call me and let me know. Will you do it?" Kate said, scrawling her number down for the umpteenth time.

"I can do that," he said, looking down at the number as he closed his front door.

By the time they reached the last house on Pear Street, two hours had gone by and still no new information.

"Should we retrace our steps and stop at the houses that were empty this morning as we make our way to Acorn?" Kate said.

"I think that's a wise idea," Arthur said. It was 3:30 pm and Kate's feet hurt. They had been walking all day, but she didn't want to stop. Like Adam had said, the next house may be the house they get what they need from. But it wasn't. It was another elderly lady in pastels. She didn't remember the disappearance and Arthur reminded them she probably didn't remember much of anything these days because of her apparent age.

"Maybe we should call it a day," Adam said with a yawn. Kate agreed; her body was tired.

"We'll pick up here tomorrow," he said and then Kate yawned.

"Interesting, the yawn," Arthur noted. "When one person yawns and the next merely *hears* the yawn, then they too are caught up in the jaw-locking phenomenon."

Kate had never thought much about a yawn, though it did seem obvious that they were quite contagious. Leave it to Arthur to be intrigued by the small things.

"So what kind of work were you doing in the courthouse for your class?" Kate asked, suddenly curious.

For the rest of the ride to Celia's apartment Arthur delved into property laws for NC and how he had been assigned to complete a map of the area as it would have been in the 1900s by tracing the ownership of the parcels of land back to that time. He explained how difficult it was to create a shape of the land parcel by reading old-time descriptions and deciphering how many feet were in 'metes' and 'bounds' which are the units of measurement for land.

When they pulled up in Celia's driveway, Arthur, who had been talking nonstop, changed his subject.

"Celia is still not home. I suppose she'll be getting here around eight. Do you have a key?"

"Yes," Kate said. She opened the door and got out while Arthur did the same to take the front seat. The chilly wind had picked up and so she dashed for the front door. Before she could turn around to wave goodbye, the car was already pulling out of the driveway.

She fumbled with the keys, trying to find the right one in the waning light and dropped them. Bending over to pick them up she noticed a bright white piece of paper near the bottom of the bushes. She reached into the prickly under part of the bush to get it. The paper was small and judging by the torn edges, it once belonged to a much bigger piece. It was blank and Kate was about to take it inside to throw it away when she turned it over and noticed words that were scrawled in pencil. The writing was very messy and she could barely read it. Some words were misspelled and the tear lines cut into others. What she could read was:

want you to know it. He treats you bad and you desserve more. What could he posbly give you? I could give you everything. And I love you. Does he love you, does he *really* love you? He wont even get you a

She wondered who the letter was intended for. Obviously it was someone reaching for the affection of someone else who was already taken. For a brief moment she entertained the idea that it might have belonged to Celia, but quickly brushed it away. And even if it had belonged to Celia, then it was quite obvious she had no intention of breaking up with Arthur for whoever wrote the letter because the letter had been torn to pieces and carelessly lost in the bushes.

She crumpled the piece of letter up and stuck the key in the door handle. Once inside she had to wrestle with the key to get it back out of the door. After a brief pause to take in the silence of the house, she went upstairs to the bedroom. She threw the wad of paper into the trash can beside the night stand and plopped down on the bed, lying back to stretch.

She started thinking about all the people they had visited that day and how they were no closer to finding what happened to Loraine than anyone else had ever been. But perhaps the trip wasn't a waste, she had Adam now; or at least maybe. She lifted up off the bed enough to pull her phone out of her pocket. There was only one way to find out.

'What happens when we get back?' she typed, then hit send.

She waited and waited, but there was no answer so Kate just lay there on the bed, daydreaming about what might have happened if she had said yes to Adam in the first place when he had come to ask her to the prom. She wondered what Abby would have said and done.

In her day dream she imagined Abby being happy for her and helping her to find the perfect dress and shoes. But a pain in her chest reminded her that the chances of that happening were slim. Now what? Did a kiss in a truck and some sweet-nothing texts constitute cheating? Did it mean she was stealing her best friend's boyfriend? He wouldn't have been her boyfriend if it weren't for Kate. Or would he have?

'What do u want to hapn?' The text she received some twenty minutes later said.

What she wanted was to be with Adam and for Abby to be OK with it. No, what she wanted was for Abby to never have even liked Adam in the first place. She needed advice, but unfortunately the one person who she wanted advice from was the one person who she needed the advice about. She didn't know how to respond to the text. She wanted to tell him she wanted to be with him, but she couldn't do that. Maybe her mom would be able to help her out. She thought about that for a moment and then decided that including her mother in on anything in her private life might not be a good idea. Her mother had a tendency to limit her with rules and she didn't want to be told exactly what to do with the expectation that she do it the way she was told to do it. She wanted opinions with the freedom to decide if she would take the advice or not. So mom was out of the decision. What about Cora? She had dialed half of Cora's number when she got a new text from Adam.

'I want 2 b w u, not Abby,' it read. For a moment she wondered if he had been talking to Abby every night. It made her jealous to think that he might be on the phone with her now.

'I know' she texted back. And she didn't know what to do, but she was definitely tired of stepping aside to let Abby have the limelight. This time, she wouldn't do it; she deserved to be with the person she wanted most and that person was Adam.

On a whim she texted, "come c me.' She wanted nothing more at the moment than to be near him.

She laid her phone on her chest and put her hands behind her head, waiting for a return text. She lay in the bed, staring above and noticed two words stenciled on the ceiling. Shifting and turning her body, she was able to read, 'sweet dreams'. It was stenciled in the place above the bed where whoever was sleeping in it would be able to read it if they had their head on the pillow and was looking straight up at it. She would steal that idea for her own dorm room in a few years. At twenty past seven she wondered if Adam had fallen asleep or if he had been on the phone with Abby because she hadn't received a text back. It had been almost fifteen minutes.

CHAPTER EIGHT

There was a knock at the door. She sat up and wondered if she should answer it or not. Of course it would be for Celia, but Celia wasn't home from class yet. The knock sounded again and she quietly walked down the stairs, still trying to decide if she should answer it or not. Again they knocked. So she grabbed the knob quickly and opened it up wide.

It was Adam.

"Safety 101, never open your door completely to a stranger. Safety tip two, always use the chain lock to decipher how wide to open your door. Safety tip three, use the safety chain," he said, leaning up against the jamb.

"Reality check, you're not a stranger," she said, walking away from the door as he stepped in.

"You couldn't have known that," he said, closing the door and taking off his black leather jacket.

Kate sat in the corner of the sofa and turned the TV on with the remote. Adam sat beside her.

"I didn't expect you to show up," she said, grinning.

"You asked me to," he said, shrugging.

Kate got his drift. He wanted to do anything she wanted him to do. He would do anything for her. No one in her whole life had ever been like that with her and it made her happy. It made her heart swell inside her chest and she couldn't speak. She felt like she mattered to someone other than her mother.

"Didn't you?" He asked, looking at her now.

"Yeah, I did," she said. He rested his arm on the knee that she had propped up in front of her. It only made her want to be nearer to him, so she let her knee fall and she moved closer to him, putting her head on his shoulder. He let his head softly fall onto hers as she began flipping through the channels with her right hand. Adam laced his fingers into her left hand and she smiled. They watched an episode of King of the Hill. It was the episode where Buckley breaks up with Luanne and Luanne is so upset she cries for days so Hank tries to find her a new boyfriend.

"That's what we can do for Abby," Adam said, smiling. It was an attempt to bring humor to the situation.

Kate chuckled.

"That could work," she said.

"Maybe Dewy Monty," he said with a grin.

Dewy Monty wasn't the most likely character for Abby. He had been the stinky kid in grade school and had become very eccentric in their high school years. He once brought molded cheese in for show in tell when they were younger. In eighth grade he tried to see how many pebbles he could stuff up his nose during outside break. His latest stunts had evolved to high school level. They involved inhalants. Dewy Monty had the worst GPA in the history of Change Modei High. Even though he was a year older than Adam and Kate, he was still a freshman. They imagined he'd be in high school for the rest of his life.

Kate gave Adam a dirty look for suggesting him.

"What? She'd be good for him," he said, shrugging.

"I was thinking more like James Johnson," she said. James was the running back for their school's football team. He was tall, muscular and smart.

"Boooo, that's just boring," Adam said, moving to put his arm around Kate. She settled her head into the spot where his arm connected to his chest and wrapped her arm across his waist.

"Abby needs to use her popularity to better people, to uplift the general population. All those poor ugly people," Adam joked, shaking his head.

"That's mean," Kate said, giggling.

"Mean? How's it mean?"

Kate rolled her eyes as she felt his chest bobble with laughter. They were quiet for a while as they watched Hank attempt to find Louann a new boyfriend. Toward the end of the show, Kate could feel her eyelids getting heavy. She didn't want to fall asleep, she didn't want Adam to leave and so she fought it. A second episode of King of the Hill was coming on when she felt Adam move underneath her. For a moment she thought he was getting up to leave, but instead he stretched himself out across the couch.

"Come up here," he said, pulling Kate to the inside, positioning her in between him and the back of the couch. They lay side by side.

"What about when Celia comes home?" She asked, sleepily.

"Celia was already at Arthur's when I left. I imagined they wanted to be alone."

"Do they--" Kate started to ask, but then stopped.

Adam chuckled and said, "Yeah, I'm sure they do."

"Does he tell you about it?" She asked, smiling.

"Perhaps," he said with a large grin on his face.

"What does he tell you?" She asked.

But Adam only laughed.

"You're not going to tell me?" She asked, looking up into his face, still smiling.

"Well, it's kind of, you know. He just tells me what they try, that kind of stuff," he said.

"Have you?" She asked, surprising herself. It really wasn't a question she wanted an answer to, but the curiosity was too much.

"Um," Adam started, pursing his lips together. He was trying to think of a way to answer that question. "Not entirely."

"So you've messed around then?" She asked.

"Yeah, but nothing big. Not…you know," he answered.

And now she was sorry she had asked. She wondered if he had messed around with Abby. Three weeks wasn't a long time to be with someone, but she knew they definitely had plenty of opportunities. She wanted to ask, 'with Abby?' but she knew better. She did not want to know.

"Just so you know, not with Abby," he said.

"How do you *do* that?" She exclaimed.

"I'm not sure, like I said, I can't do it with anyone else. But it's not like I'm reading your mind or anything. I don't know how to explain it. I just figure it out."

Kate looked up into his face again and he kissed her forehead, letting his lips linger on her skin for a few moments. Kate's eyes closed and she breathed in his scent. Warmth traveled across the inside of her eyelids and a smile spread across her face. When his lips left her skin, she kept her eyes closed, committing it to memory. She could feel the rise and fall of his chest as he breathed. After a few moments she noticed his breathing slowed and sleep overcame her.

She had been asleep for hours when her phone rang. It buzzed so hard that it walked itself across the table to the edge. Kate's eyes popped open with the first loud ring and the buzzing was so incessant that she crawled over Adam, who awoke and stirred under her outstretched body. Reaching as far as she could she was barely able to grab the phone before it fell over the side of the table. Looking at the screen she saw it was a number she didn't recognize. She also saw that it was almost two in the morning. Who would be calling her at two in the morning? For a moment she worried something must be wrong with her mother.

"Hello?" She said into the phone with a sleeper's voice.

"Is this Kate?" The male voice asked, slurring his words together. Immediately she knew the person had been drinking.

"Yeah, this is Kate. Who is this?"

"This is David. Sorry to call you so late, but I think I have some information you'll want and I was afraid I might forget it tomorrow," then he chuckled and continued. "I'm a little bit, uh, well, drunk so I need to tell you now." Kate sat up fully and forced her brain to wake up completely.

"Who is it?" Adam whispered to her.

Kate dropped the phone to her chin and mouthed, 'David' hoping Adam would remember the name. She remembered him from earlier that day. He had been the only person who had actually known Loraine, well, knew her at least a little bit.

"I was at a bonfire tonight and some girls I went to high school with showed up. We were talking about old times, you know, the good ole days. And one of them brought up this kid that was slow. You know, like, stupid. They were talking about how one time one of 'em's brother convinced the kid to eat dog poop and I don't know why I didn't think about it before, but then I remembered you asking about if there was anyone got made fun of a lot, someone lots of people picked on. Is this something useful or am I just making a useless drunk phone call?"

Kate thought for a moment. Was this the boy that Nabhanya had told her to look for? Or was this just a coincidence?

"What is his name?" Kate asked him.

"Lane Delaney. We called him Laney Delayed. So am I helpful?" He asked.

"Yes, yeah that's definitely helpful. Do you know where I can find him?"

"Back then he lived in the trailer park on Montgomery Boulevard with his mother or his grandmother or something like that. Most the kids that were mean to him lived in the trailer park, too, but I don't think he lives there anymore. At least I've not seen him around any."

"Do you know anyone who would know how to reach him?"

"Naw, I don't think I do. Why would you be looking for that sort of person anyway? What's it got to do with that girl's disappearing?" He asked.

"Probably nothing, but just a few things we need to check into," Kate answered, not revealing where she had gotten the hint.

"Oh, well, I hope you find what you need. I think I'm going to go say hello to the porcelain god. I'll talk to you later," he said. Kate wondered what he meant by 'porcelain god'.

She clicked her phone off and looked over her shoulder at a waiting Adam.

"He said he remembered a kid who was made fun of a lot. He said his name was Lane Delaney and they called him Laney Delayed," she said. Looking ahead of her into the dark living room she remembered the dream she had had a few weeks ago. She recalled a boy that was 'slow' trying to tell her that Abby was no longer alive. And then things began to piece together as she remembered the second dream that involved a developmentally delayed boy.

Adam sat up and put his hand on her shoulder blade.

"Are you OK, Kate?" He asked.

Kate put her hands to her temples, she was shocked. She had been dreaming about this boy the whole time.

"Ohmigosh, Adam," she exasperated.

"What?"

"Ohmigosh," she said again, this time her hands covering her mouth. Could it possibly be?

"I've been having these dreams where a boy, well, he's not really a boy in my dream but he acts like one because he's developmentally delayed. I've had two dreams with him in it," she explained. And then it all made sense. She recalled Nabhanya's description of the boy and knew that it was the person she was meant to look for.

"Adam, I already know what he looks like, or looked like anyway, I'm not sure," she said.

"Can you draw?" Adam asked.

"I wish I could, it would be so helpful. But unfortunately I was *not* born with that gift," she said.

"Well, did he know where we could find him?"

Kate told Adam about the boy living in the trailer park and how David didn't know where to find him.

"Well, we'll start there tomorrow. I don't think Arthur would be able to help us using his mad courthouse parcel look-up skills though. I'm certain one person would have owned the trailer park lots and rented them out," Adam explained.

"You're probably right," Kate said.

"So I guess the only way to do it is to visit every single resident in the park and ask them if they remembered him or knew how to get in touch with him," he said, shrugging.

"Maybe if we found his exact address there would be a forward to address listed with the postal service," Kate said.

"Possibly."

Kate could tell Adam was still mostly asleep. Now, after the shock of realizing she might know exactly what the boy looked like, she was beginning to get sleepy again as well.

"Want to go upstairs and sleep in the bed?" She asked. She had no intention of doing anything sexual with Adam, she just wanted to sleep beside him.

"What?" Adam asked with a light chuckle. "I didn't mean like that, I meant to just sleep," she said.

"Right," Adam said with a smile.

"I'm serious. There's more room." Then with a smile she added, "think you can handle it?"

"Can *you* handle it?" Adam said.

"Oh I don't know, you're pretty irresistible," she teased.

Adam swung his legs over the side of the couch, stood and stretched his arms toward the ceiling. After a big yawn he looked back at Kate. As Kate stood, Adam took her hand and led her upstairs. Suddenly she was nervous. Had she given him the wrong idea? Honestly all she wanted was to just sleep beside him. Hopefully he didn't think she was just saying that.

Halfway up the stairs she stopped. Feeling the release of her hand Adam turned back to look at her from a few stairs up.

"Um, I really don't want that. Not yet, I mean. I mean, I just want…" she tried to explain.

"Relax, Kate. I get it," he said.

Of course he gets it, Kate thought, *he practically reads my mind.* As she entered the room she turned the light on. Adam crawled into the bed and pulled the blanket up to his chest. With his arms behind his head he looked on at Kate with a smile.

"Why are you smiling at me like that?" She asked him as she dug through her bag for pajama pants and a toothbrush.

"Two reasons. One, you're cute. Two, I never imagined this would actually happen. Here, with you. Hurry up already, I want you right here," he said, patting the pillow beside him.

Kate was smiling so big that she forced herself to hide it by turning her back and pretending to rummage through her bag some more. After pulling out her toothbrush and pajamas she headed into the bathroom on the landing, just outside the bedroom door.

She turned the water on and stood looking at her smiling face in the mirror. She was perfectly content. She had Adam. And right now she just wanted to enjoy that because she knew once they got back they'd have to tell Abby. Her stomach became upset. She sighed, put paste on her toothbrush and started brushing her teeth.

I mean I can't keep stepping aside, this is what I want. What about what I want? She was saying to herself.

Why did Abby have to choose him anyway? There are tons of perfectly goodlooking, smart guys at our school. She could have her pick of any of them! And yet she has to choose the one person that I want.

Spitting into the sink she saw she had made her gums bleed from scrubbing her teeth too hard. Running her tongue over her gums she could feel the abrasions. She'd regret it in the morning; it was certainly going to be sore.

By the time Kate returned to the bedroom Adam had already fallen asleep. Crawling in beside him should seem awkward to her, but it wasn't awkward at all. Even though prior to two weeks ago they had only said 'hi' to one another in the hallways, it felt like she had known him for a really long time. Technically she had known him since sixth grade, but she had never known him like she knew him now. Why had she waited so long to talk to him?

She lifted the blanket and settled into the bed with her back toward him. After a moment she felt Adam roll toward her and wrap his arm around her with his chest resting against her back. The night was perfect. Not even a good tip to finding Loraine topped that moment. It wasn't long before she happily drifted off to sleep.

CHAPTER NINE

In the morning when she awoke, Adam was gone. At first she thought he had just moved to the other side of the bed, but when she rolled over there was no one there. She sat up, wondering why he had left. She got quickly out of the bed and peeked out onto the landing to see if the bathroom door was closed, which would mean he was using it. But it was wide open. Celia's bedroom door was open as well. She went down the stairs and from halfway she could see that the living room was empty as well. But as she reached the bottom stair she smelled a waft of a coffee aroma and heard someone sniffling in the kitchen.

In the kitchen there was Adam. He was leaning against the counter, stirring a cup of coffee. He looked up at her and smiled.

"Good morning, sleepy head. Want coffee?"

"You sound terrible," she said.

Adam's voice had grown scruffy and his eyes were puffy. Every few minutes he would sniffle.

"Yeah, I think I got a cold," he said.

"Maybe you should go back upstairs and lie down," she suggested.

"Nah, I'll be fine. It sounds worse than it feels," he said. "Besides, we got some work to do today. Time is running out."

Kate hadn't forgotten about the phone call they got last night. She could remember every word of it, but she wondered if trying to find Lane Delaney was going to lead to anything. What if Arthur was right and Nabhanya wasn't really seeing anything, just guessing? *I mean, every town everywhere has bullies and bullied kids,* she thought. Somewhere in the back of her mind though she scolded herself for second guessing Nabhanya and the intense feelings she had the night before.

"I think we should really try to find him. I think Nabhanya wouldn't try to steer us wrong," Adam said. His tendency to be inside her head suddenly caused an eruption of irritation inside of her.

Frustrated, she said, "really? You got to stop doing that." But Adam only smiled and sipped his coffee.

"How do you even do that?" She asked him, taking a seat in one of the bar stools.

"I was thinking about how to describe that last night. The only way I can explain it is that I guess. That's all I'm doing, guessing. I just get this sense of what you might be feeling and I play it out in my head to simply guess what thoughts those feelings might create."

Adam brought the cup up to his lips to hide his smile, "and so far I've not been wrong."

Adam sat the coffee cup on the counter top and asked, "how do you take your coffee?"

"None for me," she said. "But I could go for some pancakes."

"Pancakes it is. IHop or Denny's?"

"IHop," she answered.

After a heavy breakfast of pancakes, scrambled eggs and sausage Kate leaned back in the booth. She felt ready for a nap and not even the thought of possibly finding out what happened to Loraine could pull it from her. Besides, finding what happened to Loraine felt like a joke. How in the world did she ever really think she could do it? She expected Adam to say something to encourage her to continue but he was preoccupied with the last few bites of his bacon.

"Do you think we should continue?" She asked him.

"Continue?" He asked with his mouth full. Kate cringed.

"Yeah, with trying to find out what happened to Loraine. Do you think it's a waste of time?"

"I don't think it's a waste of time. I think it's a fun adventure. And even if we don't find anything, it was still fun. I mean if 'attempting to find a missing person' were on our list of things to do before we die, then we could cross that off. Besides, we just got some good new information. Aren't you excited?"

Kate smiled. His humor was horrible, his table manners were terrible and he wouldn't blow his freaking nose. She smiled to herself, thinking it was cute. She was quickly growing a fondness for it all. Glancing up, she looked at his lips and longed for them to be on hers, after he wiped the food crumbs from his mouth of course.

"Arthur is awake," he said, interrupting her inevitable day dream. Adam had his phone out, she must not have heard it ring.

"Hello?" Adam said into the phone.

He must have turned down the volume of his phone at some point because now she couldn't hear what the person on the other end was saying. She listened to Adam telling Arthur about the phone call they received last night from David. After the conversation, Adam hung up the phone.

"Adam suggested we go see the owner of the trailer park lots and see if he has kept any type of information on previous tenants," he said to Kate.

"I love your brother," Kate said chuckling. "What would we do without him? We probably would have never even met David if it wasn't for him."

"Possibly," Adam agreed.

After picking up Arthur they drove to the trailer park. According to Arthur's findings the trailer park owner lived in the trailer park herself. Her name was Magdeline Rogers.

Kate rapped on the metal-lined door. A woman in a big, furry coat opened it. She was holding a small Chihuahua in her left arm and a cigarette in a long cigarette holder in her right. The woman reminded her of Cruella De Vil. Her bleached blonde hair was a mess of curls and her thick makeup was smudged in places. It was only nine thirty in the morning and she looked like she had just come in from a night out on the town.

Blowing smoke into the air above their heads she asked, "What?"

"Hi, Ms. Rogers, I'm Kate. I'm trying to locate someone who lived here a bit back and I'm hoping you can help me," she said.

"Are you with the police?" She asked, flicking her ashes onto the step in between them.

"No, we're not. We're looking for a Lane Delaney," Kate said.

"What on Earth would the police want with Lane Delaney?" She asked, dumping her cigarette onto the step. She licked her lips and waited for the answer.

"We're not with the police," Adam reiterated. "We're just looking for Lane. Do you know how we can get in touch with him?"

Magdeline looked down at them for a moment, considering her response.

"Of course you're not with the police, you're much too young," she decided aloud. "Lane lives out near the pond. His mother, who I never expected to live this long, cursed contract, lives in Unit 5310." Magdeline pointed to a place over their heads.

"What is the name of the pond?" Arthur asked.

"Oh, I don't know. It's some pond in Jeferton they tell me. It's about fifty miles from here I think, up this road. Go ask his mother," she said and closed the door.

The words 'the pond' echoed in her mind. She recalled the breath of hot air she felt on her ear in the dream. It had whispered "near the pond." Her intuition flooded back into her and she knew without a doubt they were on the right track.

"Boy she was hot, huh?" Arthur joked as they walked away.

"Shh," Kate sushed as she laughed at his comment, "she'll hear you."

"So," Arthur said.

"So, what if she comes up and tells us to get off her property?" Kate said.

"Then I guess we'll get off her property. I already know where Lane is living," he said.

"You do?" Kate said at the same time that Adam said, "Where?"

"In fact, I've seen him before," Arthur said.

"What does he look like?" Kate asked quickly. She was curious to know if it sounded at all like the boy in her dream. At the same time Adam said, "where at?"

Arthur decided to answer Adam's question instead.

"They say he's crazy, he lives out in the middle of nowhere by himself and shoots anyone that comes onto his property. They say he worked at a gas station for like twenty something years or something like that and when the gas station owner died and sold it to someone new, Lane went crazy and attacked the new owner. They say he ripped him apart with his bare hands. When the police found the dead owner, they said it looked like the person who had killed him had tried eating him, too. They arrested Lane and he went away to a mental institution for a few years, but they were never able to prove it was him."

Chills bloomed on Kate's flesh. Had this been a similar fate for her sister? A small sigh escaped from her lips and she had to stop walking. Images began swirling in her mind. Adam looked back at her and then smashed Arthur right in the chest, sending him stumbling a few steps back.

"What the fuck?" Arthur said, rearranging his jacket sleeve that had come off his arm.

"The hell's your problem?" Adam exclaimed, pointing down at Kate. Somehow Kate had fallen to her knees and not even realized it. She was overwhelmed by the thought of someone hurting her sister. Images flashed through her mind and she became unaware of all that was going on around her. She could hear 'it was an accident' and 'he loved her' and 'over a cliff' in her mind in Nabhanya's voice as she spaced out. And then she knew. She knew that it was Lane that had killed her sister. There was not a question about it, she knew he was the one.

"He did it," she heard herself say in a weak voice. It was her voice, she recognized it, but she felt like she was on autopilot, she felt detached from herself.

"What?" Arthur asked.

"He did it. I know he did. Loraine. I don't know how I know it, but I do," she heard herself say.

"Asshole," Adam said to Arthur. Adam put his grip under Kate's arm and pulled her to her feet. Kate's eyes were still glazed over and she stared out into nothing, unfocused. A single, warm tear rolled down her cheek, making a pathway that the coldness of the air attached to. Adam wrapped his arm around her as more tears came.

Now Arthur understood. "I'm...I'm sorry, Kate. I wasn't thinking. I shouldn't have..." Arthur said, but he couldn't find it in him to finish.

Kate wanted to say 'it's fine' and she really meant it, it wasn't Arthur's fault. But her mouth wouldn't work. More images were reeling like a movie in front of her eyes, but this time Nabhanya's voice was not present.

Arthur came to her other side and helped Adam hold her up, but just like that, the rush of emotions and images and voices vanished. She could stand on her own and her head had cleared.

"I guess we better go see him," she said, wiping her face with her hands. She hated crying, especially in front of other people.

"Maybe we should go back to the apartment and let you lie down," Arthur suggested, concerned.

"No, I'm fine now. I don't know what happened there, I just--" she said.

"You were overwhelmed probably," Arthur said. "I'm real sorry, Kate. I didn't even think about--"

"It's OK, Arthur. You couldn't have known. I didn't even know," she said, hoping to make him feel better. But her stomach was queasy and she couldn't continue what she had planned to say.

"Maybe you *should* go lie down, Kate. Arthur and I can go out and talk to Lane. It'd be safer anyway," Adam said.

"No, I'm going, too. Besides, that story is probably just an urban legend college kids made up to scare freshmen," she said, teasing Arthur, hoping to make him smile.

"You're probably right," he said through his grin. The gravel crunched under their feet as they made their way back to Arthur's car, which they had parked in the drive beside the trailer marked 'Business Office'.

As they drove down the road Adam asked her, "are you sure you want to do this right now?"

"Of course," she said, worried Adam would back out on her. "We have to go today."

"Like Adam said, we can go and you can go back to the apartment. You were pretty affected back there. It might be the better idea," Arthur said.

"No, I need to do this. I need to know if Lane had anything to do with Loraine's disappearance," she said, even though she already knew.

Adam drew in a deep breath and let it out slowly. Kate could tell her stubbornness was aggravating him.

"Fine. Then we'll need a plan. Obviously we can't just go up to him and ask him if he had anything to do with Loraine," he said.

Kate was stuck. How would she approach him? What would she say?

"Let's just ask him the same questions we've been asking everyone else. We don't want him to think we think he is guilty of something. I mean, we don't even know anything for sure," Arthur said. But Kate did know. She knew he had something to do with Loraine's disappearance. She wasn't going to argue, though, it'd be a waste of time. Besides, Arthur's idea was a good one.

They were driving down a back road, some twenty minutes outside the city. "Are you sure you know where you're going?" Adam asked.

"Yep. Some of us drove out here on Halloween, like Kate said: to give us freshmen a good scare," he explained. "We're almost there."

Outside the window Kate could see for miles. And all she saw for miles were corn fields. The land was flat and dry in the winter season. The sky was gray and dreary but it wasn't raining yet. She was accustomed to the mountainous horizon of West Virginia so the flatness of the land made her eyes feel tired. She rubbed them to get them to focus, but looking so far off into the distance made them hurt.

Arthur slowed the truck and pulled to the side of the dusty, gravel road.

"There it is," he said, squinting out the front windshield.

Kate, who was sitting in the backseat, leaned forward. Up ahead she could see the road take a sharp, right turn as a wooded area began. Just in the crook of the turn was a gravel driveway that was silhouetted by large trees on both sides. The driveway curved off to the left and they weren't able to see beyond it because of all the trees.

"Did you guys go all the way up to it?" Kate asked, now worried about the part of the legend where Lane would shoot any trespassers.

"No, we stopped here," Arthur said to her dismay. He put the car in gear again and continued the drive up to the eerie wooded area. The car became dark as they drove into the wooded area, so dark it was almost like a night with a full moon. It didn't help that Arthur had slowed his driving. It was like he expected something to jump out from the brush. They all sat, wide-eyed, watching the large tree branches and brushes go by out the window.

Finally they reached the foot of the driveway and Arthur turned into it. They went around the corner and Kate pictured what it must have looked like from the point on the road where they had stopped earlier. She imagined they must have looked like a slow-moving car disappearing into the unknown.

Now that they had come around the corner Kate could see an old, run-down house. To the left was a pond with a dock, all surrounded by woods. Fallen leaves surrounded the pond so densely that it looked like the area around the pond was marshy. All the leaves were a shade darker than they would have been if they were dry. The rain that had fallen recently changed the the bark on the trees to a darkened color, too. They all sat in the silence and looked around them. It felt like they were waiting for someone to jump out and scare them. Kate noticed there were no cars in the driveway. She also noticed Adam nudge Arthur, who nudged Adam back. It took her a few moments, but she realized they were silently arguing over who was going to go to the door. So Kate opened her back seat door and got out. Both boys scrambled to undo their seat belts. By the time they were out of the car, Kate was already at the door, knocking loudly. Any movement that might have been going on inside the house would have been muffled by the boys running through the wet leaves toward her. When they reached her and flanked her sides she knocked again, even harder this time. Adam and Arthur had the same idea at the same time and they both banged on the door with their fists. They waited and waited and waited, but no one came to the door.

"I don't think he's home," Kate said, almost relieved.

Arthur jumped from the side of the small porch they had been standing on and walked to the corner of the house. Adam and Kate waited and watched Arthur look out over the small pond and into the back part of the property.

Kate was struggling to keep an eye on Arthur, she didn't want him to go into the backyard alone and to her relief, he never went past the corner of the house. When he began walking back toward them she sighed and turned to Adam, but Adam was not there. Panic rose up in her. Where had Adam gone? She quickly realized the front door had been opened and she saw the last glimpse of Adam's foot disappear around the door.

"Adam!" She yelled, opening the screen door. She hadn't heard him even open it. She scrambled to push the inside door open a little more so she could get through. Once inside the house she could see that it looked like no one had been there in ages. There was molded bread on the counter, flies surrounding the dishes in the sink and a layer of dust that was so thick it gave everything a gray tint.

"Adam?" She called. But no one answered. She left the kitchen and was entering the living room as she heard what she assumed to be Arthur coming in the front door.

"Adam?" She called again. There was a long hallway with two closed doors on the right, one on the left and an open bedroom door at the end. She crept slowly down the hall as she heard Arthur coming into the living room. In the bedroom with the open door, a shadow was playing on the wall opposite the wall that couldn't be seen. She imagined it was Adam so she quickened her pace. As she reached the door, she turned to the wall that couldn't be seen from the hallway. There was no one there.

"Adam?" She called once more. She turned around and ran smack into the thick chest of someone who loomed tall above her. Instantly she knew it was Lane and she screamed as loud as she could, shrunk herself down to her knees and cowered into the corner with her arms over her face.

In the distance, down the hall she could hear someone laughing. Kate began to cry and peered through her fist up into the face of the man who was about to kill her. She saw deep, brown eyes that made her feel warm. She recognized them somehow, she knew them. She expected the figure to start hitting her or dragging her away by her hair, but as she peeled her hands back further she realized where she knew the eyes from. It was Adam. Adam was laughing hysterically and so was Arthur down the hall.

"It's just me," he said, helping her to her feet again. She play punched him in the chest over and over again, but he wrapped his arms around her and pulled her in close. She gave into the hug and wrapped her arms around him tight.

"You're such a meathead," she said through a grin.

"Meathead?" Adam asked.

"Yeah, the both of you. Meatheads," she said, rolling her eyes.

While still chuckling, Arthur said, "Well, obviously no one is home. And there's nothing here to indicate when he'll be back."

"I don't think he's been here for a really long time, actually," Kate said. She brought the molded bread and dust to their attention.

"It doesn't look totally abandoned though," Adam said. "I found a toothbrush in the bathroom. No one leaves for any length of time without their toothbrush. Do they?"

Adam grasped the knob of the only door they hadn't opened. He pulled it open quickly and a gust of cold air blew in his face, bringing with it the stench of decaying animal.

"Whoa, what is that smell?" He said to them. And the smell hit Kate's nose and she had to cover it. It was a very strong, putrid smell.

But it didn't stop Adam who said, "It's a basement." He stepped down onto the first step leading down into it. Kate stood behind Arthur and could see a light on at the bottom of the stairs. Arthur followed Adam and Kate was behind him.

"Uh, maybe Kate shouldn't come down here," Adam called up to them when he reached the bottom. Kate was already halfway down the stairs and hearing someone say she shouldn't go down there only made her want to see it even more.

Arthur stopped in front of her and bent down to peer into the room where Adam was standing.

"Yeah, Kate, why don't you wait upstairs?" He agreed.

"Oh please," she countered, and pushed past Arthur. When she reached the bottom of the stairs and turned to find Adam what she saw was disgusting.

Hanging from a large hook in the ceiling was the carcass of a large deer. Its stomach had been sliced open and the guts lay on the basement floor. The smell of the rotting carcass was so strong that Kate began dry heaving. It was the worst smell in the world.

"Oh gross!" Arthur said, covering his mouth and nose with his jacket sleeve.

"Who guts a deer in their basement?" Adam asked through the sleeve he was covering his mouth and nose with.

"Lane does. He's mentally handicapped," Kate managed to say.

"We better get out of here in case he comes back soon," she said. And just as she did they all heard footsteps running up to the front porch and crashing through the front door.

They were all silent, listening to him stomp in and out of the rooms above them. Kate wondered what would happen when he realized they were in the basement. Looking around, all Kate could see were large knives and sharp utensils. From her dreams she knew the man above them that was tearing his house apart looking for them, was a very tall and strong man who could easily overpower all three of them.

Adam scurried over to the window and tried opening it as they heard a gruff, slow voice calling out into the house.

"Who's in here?" It called.

With a big push Adam was able to lift the window wide enough for them all to get out of it. Adam went first, pushing his arms and head out the window. The window was at ground level so Adam was able to slither onto the land without making much noise. Kate went next. Before she popped her head out of the hole she could hear the footsteps opening the door to the basement. She hoped they'd be able to pull Arthur out in time.

She reached her arms up and Adam pulled her the rest of the way out of the window. They were standing up as Arthur's head emerged. Adam grabbed one arm and Kate the other, but that wasn't working out so well. Arthur shrugged them off and pulled himself out of the window just as they heard footsteps on the basement stairs. Adam shut the window with a small thud and they ran toward the car.

"Wait!" Kate said, stopping.

"We can't just leave, he's seen our car," she said and she headed back to the house. If they left he would know someone had been in his house and he would know what their vehicle looked like. She couldn't help but imagine Arthur driving around in the vehicle and the man recognizing it. He might try to hurt Arthur, like he had the gas station owner, if that story were even true.

Adam looked at Arthur and Arthur looked at Adam and then they ran to catch up to Kate.

"Kate, wait," they whispered in a yelling fashion. "Kate, come back, we got to get out of here," Arthur whispered.

But Kate was already knocking on the door again. She knew Lane was there, but that it might take a bit for him to make his way back up from the basement. The boys made it to her side and began pulling her back down the porch steps.

"What are you doing?" Adam cried.

"Are you crazy?" Arthur said.

But Kate fought against them and was trying to make her way back to the door.

"He's already seen our car," she tried to explain again. "He knows we're here."

"Did you *not* see the deer in the basement? What makes you think he wouldn't do that to *us*?" Arthur said, pulling her back.

"It's not *human* meat," Kate argued. "Oh, stop it. Big babies," she said and jerked her arms from them. They both relinquished her as they heard the door at the top of the porch open. A big, burly man in overalls flew open the screen door. It shot out and bounced off the side of the house, hitting the man's big arms and bouncing back against the house again.

Kate looked up at the man. In his face she saw the boy that had been in her dreams. It was unmistakably him. A wave of trembles radiated through her body from her head to her feet and then vanished. She was looking him in the eye and she saw shear anger. Both boys were silent. She watched as the man's face went from anger to softness and then to…fear.

"Ghost," he said rather softly. Quickly he scrambled back into the house and locked his door. She could see him peering out at them through the door's window.

"Go away, ghost!" He said.

"Ghost?" Arthur said.

The three of them looked around at each other and behind them to see what he could be mistaken for a ghost.

"I think he's trying to trick us," Adam said. That made sense, the man was developmentally delayed so it made sense that he would attempt to convince them there was a ghost so they'd leave. Is that what he was doing?

"There are no ghosts," Kate said to him. She felt sorry for him, she wanted to help him. His face quickly disappeared from the door window and he screamed as loud as he could.

"Go away!"

He screamed it over and over again.

"Let's go," Kate said, realizing they were frightening him.

They all climbed into the car and Arthur made no hesitation about turning the car around and speeding back down the driveway. Before she knew it, they were back on the gravel road, passing the endless corn fields on both sides.

No one said anything until they got back into town.

"Well, that was a bust," Adam said.

"I think we scared him more than he scared us," Kate said. "Maybe we should go back and apolo--"

"Are you crazy?" Arthur cried, looking back at her. At the same time Adam yelped, "Hell no."

Kate couldn't help but laugh at their apparent fear.

"Omigosh, he's just a man. Did you see that poor look on his face?" She asked.

"Yeah, and I hope it's a face we never see again!" Arthur said. Kate rolled her eyes.

"I'm hungry," Adam said. Kate looked at the dashboard and saw that it was almost noon. She was definitely not hungry, but when they stopped at a Burgerking she went in with them.

She averted her eyes as Adam tore through a Whopper sandwich. Staring down at her own chicken sandwich she began to think about the sincerely scared look on Lane's face. No delayed individual could pull off a fake scare face like that. Lane really was scared of something. And then she realized it. Ghost. Lane had screamed 'ghost' and 'go away'. She remembered the lady at the library telling her she looked a lot like Loraine. It made sense to her. Lane thought she was Loraine's ghost. Is that possible? They weren't even able to find out if Lane knew Loraine. She opened her mouth to tell Adam and Arthur, but she decided not to tell them. She knew it was something she needed to do on her own, but she didn't have a vehicle. A plan quickly developed in her mind. She decided she'd get Adam to stay over again and when he was good and asleep she would drive his truck out to Lane's. She would talk to him alone. She knew it was something she had to do and she wouldn't be able to do it with Adam and Arthur there. They didn't seem to understand Lane, they were frightened of him. But when she had looked into his eyes, she saw something different. She saw someone who was strong, someone who was giving and caring. Thinking back to the basement she had seen an animal carcass that had been carefully dismantled. Every part of it had a use. Somehow everything was coming together for her and she understood the phrases, 'it was an accident' and "he loved her.' Though 'over a cliff' was still a loner phrase. She knew that whatever had happened was an accident and that Lane had cared for Loraine. And she had to find out if all that she was feeling was true or if she was making things up in her mind.

Kate ate half her sandwich and was ready to go. Adam was stuffing a last bite into his mouth. Arthur, on the other hand, had only made it halfway through his burger. She noticed how neatly he ate compared to his brother. He took small bites and chewed each bite decisively. She wondered if he counted his chews and only swallowed his food after a certain number had been reached. And Arthur, unlike Adam, chewed with his mouth closed and never said a word when he was chewing. How had one picked up manners and the other not?

"By the way, where's Celia?" She asked Arthur.

He swallowed his food and answered, "She went home for the rest of the weekend."

Kate got the feeling Celia didn't like her. They had never mentioned Celia going home for the rest of the weekend before; it must have been a spontaneous decision. She could see Adam look up at her, but he said nothing.

"So what should we do now?" Adam asked.

"We could see a movie," Arthur said.

"It's Sunday, matinee prices," Kate added.

"Why spend money when you can watch a movie at home?" Arthur suggested.

"Because when we do that it's usually a documentary," Adam groaned.

"I got one you'll like this time. Guaranteed."

Adam rolled his eyes.

"A documentary on what?" Kate asked.

Arthur sat up straight, looked at his brother and smiled knowingly at him. "Monster Trucks," he said.

Adam gave his brother a side glance and then pursed his lips as if he were thinking.

"I'm sure Kate wouldn't enjoy that," he said. He looked right up at Kate to see her reaction.

"Actually, I wouldn't mind. I like monster trucks," she said. And it was true, she did enjoy the shows. She had never been to a real one before, but she had occasionally stopped on the TV channels that were showing monster truck shows.

Arthur took another bite of burger and Adam grinned from ear to ear.

"Monster Trucks it is," he said.

"Then afterward we can watch the one on black holes," Arthur said quickly. But Adam rolled his eyes again.

"Kate and I should probably hit the road after. It's a long drive," he said.

So it was over. They were out of time, at least for this weekend. Adam was right, they could always come back on another weekend and try again. At least they had a lead and Kate somehow *knew* Lane was the answer.

After lunch they went to Arthur's dorm, grabbed a few movies and headed to Celia's apartment. Kate watched half of the first documentary before falling asleep. She slept for what seemed like minutes. When she awoke she could hear someone snoring. Looking over, she could see Adam's head bent backward over the top of the couch, his mouth wide open. Arthur, in the chair, was also asleep. She picked up her phone and saw that it was almost 4:00 p.m. She had slept for nearly three hours. Looking out the window she realized it was pouring rain. It pattered heavily on the roof. Kate always slept best when it was raining. She wondered how long they all had been asleep.

Now is my chance, she thought.

CHAPTER TEN

Kate got up from her spot very slowly. Adam's hand had rested on her hip and she didn't want to wake him. She looked around for the keys to the car, hoping they weren't in Arthur's pocket. To her relief they were sitting right on the coffee table along with both Adam and Arthur's cell phones. She picked the keys up with a little jingle and walked softly to the door. Opening it without making any sound would not be easy. The door was already hard to open.

She wrapped her hand around the knob and twisted it as far as it would go before pulling on it. As the seal broke it made a slight sucking noise, but neither boy was affected by the sound. She quickly pulled the door open enough to slide out of it and closed it as quietly as possible. She stood on the porch in the pouring rain. She ran to the driver's side of Arthur's car. She wished she had figured out which key it was before she decided to go out into the rain. She was drenched by the time she found the right key and was able to get into the car. She turned the heat on and shivered. Her teeth were chattering and her hair was stuck to her face.

"I'm coming, Loraine," she said as she put the car in reverse and backed out of the driveway. Now she was free to do it her way. She was going to find out what happened to her sister all those years ago and she knew it. She could feel it. She knew Lane knew everything. She could hear Nabhanya's voice in her head. "Don't go, don't go, don't go," it said. She got the feeling Nabhanya was frightened. But not even Nabhanya was going to stop her from finding out for sure and certain what happened to Loraine.

The rain was coming down so hard it made it difficult to find the right roads to turn onto. Twice she had to turn around on the interstate by using the ramps. She had hoped she'd be able to get out to Lane's house, talk to him and be back before the boys even woke up.

Finally she was going the right way and as the interstate's traffic began to disperse she took a ramp onto the county road she was looking for. She drove for what felt like forever before she finally reached the familiar corn fields that went on endlessly on both sides of the road. The flatness of the land made her eyes water and feel funny again.

Up ahead she could see where the woods began and the road twisted into it. She also noticed a big patch of fog making its way across the gravel road. Once she passed the first few trees the sunlight became scarce. The rain had turned to a drizzle, but there was so much fog it was hard to see twenty feet ahead of her. The driveway was dark as she pulled onto the gravel.

She could hear her breath becoming shallow as she turned the corner in the driveway. Up ahead loomed the house she had been in earlier that day. She remembered the dead animal carcass in the basement and how it had been torn to pieces. She also remembered how it looked like it had been done with care and precision. She tried to remind herself that Lane was a person, just like her. He wasn't a murderer, she didn't think.

She opened the door and stepped out onto the wet leaves. The whole forest was dripping with its recent rainwater. The sun was lower in the sky than she had hoped, so she made her way to the front porch quickly. She knocked on the door with four short raps. She heard a kitchen chair pushed back and large, heavy footsteps coming to the door. The door was ripped open quickly and there stood Lane. Anger had been on his face, just like earlier, but was soon replaced with fear.

"Go, go, go away!" He cried and backed up further into his kitchen.

"I'm not a ghost, Lane," she said through the screen door. But he had turned and ran deeper into the house.

Kate opened the screen door and stepped inside.

"Lane!" She called out. "Lane, I'm not a ghost. I'm not Loraine. I'm her sister, Kate. Please come out and talk to me."

She could see into the living room from the front door. She could see Lane was huddling behind a Christmas Tree he hadn't taken down, even though it was February. It wasn't bare in any spots so she guessed it was a fake tree. He was crouched down behind it, holding his knees in his arms. She felt really bad for him, he was scared.

"Lane, I know you're scared. I know I look like Loraine, but I'm not. I'm not a ghost. I just want to talk to you. Please," she said, letting her voice transition into calm as she finished her sentence. She remembered that sometimes it's easy to calm someone down just by calming one's own voice.

"No," he said covering his mouth. "Go away." She could see tears falling down his cheeks.

Kate walked toward the living room to get a little closer to him.

"Lane, I'm not here to hurt you. I'm here to help you," she said. She didn't know what she meant, but she knew it sounded good, so she went with it.

It was a guess, based on the words she had heard from Nabhanya in her mind, but she continued, "I know it was an accident. I know you loved her."

Lane sniffled and wiped tears from his face.

"Loraine hates me now," he said. Hearing him say Loraine's name confirmed he had known her and known her well. Kate's heart skipped a beat as she realized that her intuition and Nabhanya had been right.

"Loraine doesn't hate you, Lane. Trust me. She knows it was an accident," Kate said.

"Tell me what happened," she encouraged.

"Loraine is dead!" He yelled. "Long time ago," he added, quieter.

"I know," Kate said. Kate bent to her knees to be eye level with him. She sat on her knees to seem less intimidating to him.

"Lane, what happened to Loraine?" She asked.

"No!" He yelled, covering his ears and closing his eyes tight. He began to rock back and forth.

"I know you don't like what happened, but can you please tell me?" She asked.

"No!" He yelled again and began humming to block out her voice.

Kate got to her feet, walked over to Lane and knelt beside him. She reached out slowly to take his hand from his ears. When her skin touched his he began bellowing out sounds as if he were in pain. He twisted and contorted trying to get away from her, nearly knocking over the tree before passing through to the other side of it and running off.

As Kate came around the opposite side of the tree she could see the basement door was open and could hear Lane crashing down at the stairs. He had fallen.

"Lane!" She cried as she ran over to the door that led to the basement.

Below she could see that Lane's foot had gone through one of the steps near the bottom of the stairs and he was stuck. Frantically he pulled at it, trying to get loose as Kate started down the steps to help him. Halfway down Lane stood up and began trying to run, pulling his leg as hard as he could.

"Lane, stop, you're going to hurt yourself," Kate said. But Lane didn't stop and so Kate continued down the stairs. He was turned away from her, wanting to run and she gripped his heavy, booted foot and tried wedging it out of the hole.

"Lane, you have to stop moving so I can get your foot out. Sit down," she told him. But Lane was even more frantic now; he was petrified and pulling as hard as he could to get away. He was crying and screaming.

"Lane!" She yelled loudly so he could hear her over his cries.

When he still didn't calm down again, she yelled to him again and again. She yelled to him until finally he began to calm. She imagined her standing there beside him for that long of a time made him realize she wasn't going to hurt him. Finally he was quiet except for an occasional whimper that escaped him from his sobbing.

When he was quiet enough, Lane said, "I'm not here to hurt you, Lane. I'm not here to take you away either."

"Mama said never say it," he said.

"Never say what?" Kate asked. But Lane squeezed his eyes shut tight and pursed his lips together.

"I'm going to get your foot unstuck, OK? But please don't run away. I'm not going to do anything to you," she told him. Lane sniffed back more sobs.

"Do you want me to get your foot unstuck, Lane?" She asked.

Lane shook his head without opening his eyes.

"Will you not run away?" She asked. Lane stood still for a moment and then he shook his head for no.

"I'll get your foot unstuck if you promise me you won't run. Do you promise?" She asked to be sure. Lane shook his head for yes.

"OK, sit on the stair so I can get it out," she instructed. Lane opened his eyes and looked around. Slowly he sat on the stair, deliberately not looking at Kate.

When he was seated on the stair Kate was able to get his foot at the right angle and it slipped out easily. As she lifted it out his pant leg rose up on his calf and she could see a big gash in his leg. It was bleeding profusely.

"Lane your leg is bleeding. Let's go upstairs so I can clean it and put a bandage on it," she said calmly, trying to encourage his calmness.

Lane looked down, moving his leg and trying to see his wound.

"I don't see nothing. You're tricking me," he said.

"No. Let me see your hand, I'll show you," she said. Lane offered his hand and Kate took it, put it gently on the wound so that blood would be on it and then showed it to Lane.

"It is bleeding," he said.

"Yes, it is bleeding. If we don't clean it then it will get infected and it will be painful. I don't want it to hurt you, so let's go upstairs and I will clean it for you," she said, hoping he'd agree without incident.

"You are helping?" He asked.

"Yes, I am helping," she answered. The dangerousness of the situation fell upon her. Lane was between her and the only exit out of the basement. He could easily overpower her and take her down where all the sharp knives, hammers and saws were.

"I'll go first," she said, scrambling around him and up the stairs. When she reached the top she was relieved to find he wasn't far behind her. She watched the blood drops fall onto the carpet as they walked into the kitchen. Lane sat in a chair and Kate washed her hands over the dirty sink.

"Why don't you clean your dishes, Lane?" She asked him.

"Mama does," he said.

"Where is your mama?" Kate asked him.

"She has her own house. She lives there," he answered.

"Do you have any bandages?" She asked him. When he didn't answer her she turned to him and asked the same question a second time. He was shaking his head no when she realized he must have been shaking his head the first time she had asked him.

"I'm sorry my friends and I scared you earlier today," she said to him. He looked wore out, uncared for. There was dried mud in his hair. His face and arms were gray-white with dirt. *This man should not be living on his own,* she thought.

"I thought you were a ghost," he said.

"I know you did. You thought I was Loraine's ghost, didn't you?" And Lane shook his head for yes.

Kate rummaged through the pull-out drawers along the counters to find something that was clean enough to use as a bandage. She came across a store-bought package of hand towels that were still in their cellophane packaging. She ripped open the package and turned the water to run as hot as it would go. She doused the corner of one towel in the hot water and bought it over to Lane. She knelt down at his knees and lifted his pant leg high enough so that she could wipe the blood from his leg.

"It does not hurt," he said to her.

"You're a tough guy," she said to him, to make him feel good.

"I am strong," he said with a satisfied smile.

After wiping the blood from his leg she saw that it wasn't as bad as she thought it was. It was merely scraped. It was a lot of blood from such a small scrape. She hoped he wasn't anemic or was taking blood-thinners for a medical reason.

When the blood finally began to clot she stopped wiping. She looked up at him and asked, "Do you remember Loraine?"

"I'm not supposed to talk about her," he said.

"Who told you you're not supposed to talk about her?" Kate asked.

"Mama," he said.

She was not proud about what she was about to do, but she knew it was going to be the easiest way to get it out of him.

"Your mama is probably right. You shouldn't talk about her, it upsets you. But I'm Loraine's sister. I don't have any memories of her. I never knew her. Will you tell me some things about her so I'll know something about her?" She asked.

Lane looked up over her head and out the window over the sink.

"She had dark hair. It smelled good," he began. A smile spread over his face and he closed his eyes to remember.

"She liked me. No one never liked me. The people pick on me a lot, made fun of me because I don't, I can't think like they do. I don't know why, I just never could do it. She liked me. She sat by me on the school bus and walked me home so kids wouldn't throw rocks at me. I live out here now where no one can find me to throw things at me. She never threw anything at me. She talked to me all the time wherever I went and she was there."

He opened his eyes and his body relaxed into serenity. She could tell by looking into his face that he did love her sister.

"She was nice to you when others were mean," Kate said. Lane nodded for yes.

"You must have really liked her," she said and Lane nodded for yes.

"She was my friend," he said.

"What happened to her?" She asked him, and instantly his face contorted into pain and a tear squeezed out from his eye. His lips parted and revealed the saliva that his tears had caused. His head swayed from left to right and he closed his eyes.

"I can't tell," he said.

"Did anyone come to talk to you after she was gone?" Kate asked. "Did a police officer talk to you after she disappeared?"

Lane nodded his head for no.

"Mama said not to tell because they'd take me away to a bad place and I'd never see her again," he said.

"No one's going to take you away, Lane. You can tell me. I'm her sister," she said to him. And to her amazement he began to tell her.

"I gave her a magic shot. They told me it would make her feel really good," he said.

Kate felt a dizziness that took over her. She turned her body so that her back rested against a table leg. She was beginning to space out again but this time she felt sick. Sweat began to bead on her forehead. *What is happening to me?* She thought as felt herself slipping away. Her legs were straight in front of her. She could hear his voice, but her vision began blurring in and out.

"We were friends," he said, crying.

Kate's head was filled with new images. She was in the passenger seat of a car, waking up. The radio was on. Blurred images were flying by and she understood she was looking out the passenger side window. It was gray and bleak out and the images that passed were rocky and tree-lined. She could hear Lane singing with the radio and she felt herself dry heaving, but nothing was coming up and then she faded into sleep again.

"Where did you take her?" Kate asked him, feeling very nauseous. She was suddenly very sick and very weak. But she would not stop asking him questions, this might be her only chance to find out what happened to her sister.

"For a ride. I just wanted her to be with me and not with anyone else. I wanted her with me. We ran away in my car," he said.

Kate was still feeling like she was in the passenger seat of a vehicle. She could feel the rumble and movement of the engine and she could smell burning oil.

"Where did you take her?" Kate said as sweat rolled down her face.

"For a ride," he said and now he was crying really hard.

"What happened to her Lane?" Kate asked, drenched in sweat. Her stomach was twisting into knots and she began to feel like her blood was on fire. She didn't know what was happening to her but she knew it was some kind of connection. She knew she had to keep Lane talking about Loraine so she could find out what happened. So far there wasn't anything that was making any sense.

"She wouldn't wake up," he said through his sobs.

"They said on the TV that someone kidnapped her and I knew it was me. I had her, she was with me and I was going to be in trouble. I know what happens to people who kidnap people. They are bad people. I did something bad," he cried. Now he was rocking back and forth in his chair and the tears continued to fall heavily. He covered his ears with his hands and squeezed his eyes shut tight again. His lips were pursed the same way as earlier.

"I'm bad, I'm bad, I'm bad," he kept saying as he rocked.

Kate had turned pale on the floor. She wasn't able to move and she was very hot. She didn't know what was going on with her body, but she knew she couldn't stop, not now.

"No, Lane. You're not bad. Just tell me what happened next," she said with exasperation.

"I had her and she wasn't waking up. I was going to be in trouble, lots of trouble, bad trouble. I knew she was dead. She wasn't waking up and she wasn't breathing either. Her lips were blue. I knew she was dead," he said.

"She's dead, dead, dead," he whimpered, barely audible and rocking back and forth heavily.

Kate could see it in her mind. She could see Lane stopping at a restaurant to eat, leaving Loraine in the car. She could understand that Lane thought Loraine was just asleep. She could see him eating French fries with ketchup and watching the television above the bar. She watched the news feed about the missing girl and saw the police uniforms. She watched from a distant place as Lane realized he was in trouble. She watched him pay for his lunch and watched him go out the door. She watched him pace back and forth beside the vehicle, talking to himself. He was scared. She watched him sit down beside the car and rock back and forth with his hands on his head, just as he was doing now in the kitchen.

"What did you do with her?" Kate asked, feeling sicker and sicker.

"I took her to the heights and I left her," he said through his tears. Kate knew without asking that the heights were cliffs.

Kate's mouth was dry and her tongue was sticking to the roof of her mouth. She could see flashing images of Lane pulling Loraine from the car, but she couldn't see anything past it. But she knew. She knew he had dumped her over the cliff and the last of Nabhanya's words made sense to her now.

"Did you throw her body over the cliff?" Kate asked him.

"Yes," he said, crying even more hysterically.

"I did it, I did it, I did it," He kept repeating as he rocked. Kate wanted to console him; she knew he didn't quite understand and she knew he was scared. She knew now that it was truly an accident and she could see he was hurting from having to remember it. But what had killed her? What had he done to cause her to not wake up?

"What made her sick?" Kate asked him, feeling like she might pass out.

"Mama says it was the magic shot," he said.

What was the magic shot? She wondered.

"What do you mean?" She asked him.

"The magic shot I gave her. It was to make her feel happy all the time. But mama said it killed her," he mumbled.

"Where did you get it?" She asked him.

"From the Dunbee brothers, Mike and Mark. They showed it to me at their house. They gave it to me in my arm and it made me happy. I wanted her to be happy like that. It worked for me, why didn't it work for her?"

Happy. Magic shot. Now it was coming together. It must have been some sort of drug. The boys had given him a drug. She had heard of individuals shooting stuff into their veins for highs, but she didn't know much more than that. It was a world she was unaware of, one she'd never visited.

"You put the shot in your arm?" She asked him, to show him she understood.

"Yes," he cried.

"And you gave the shot to Loraine?" She asked.

Lane calmed down a little as he concentrated on remembering. "They wanted me to take her to the pond. They told me to give her the shot and she would be happy. So I did. And I put the needle in her skin when she wasn't looking. She was happy for a while and when she started to feel bad I gave her more. We went for a ride in my car. All day we drove. And at night time we stopped and slept. But she got sick. She got really sick. And she went to sleep," and then he fell apart again. Through his sob, almost inaudible he said, "She never woke up."

Lane uncovered his eyes and slid his hands down to his cheeks. He still didn't seem to take notice that Kate was in the floor and he definitely didn't notice her physical state.

Kate could feel her lips go as dry as her mouth and she knew she was glazed over. All the energy had been sucked from her body.

Lane began to squeal again as another wave of grief passed over him. Now his head bent into his hands and he cried hard.

"She wouldn't wake up," he said.

Kate was tapped. There was nothing left in her body to ask any more questions or to try to see anything more in her mind. She tried to let go of her new found ability and to shut it off, but she imagined standing so near to Lane and hearing his pain was keeping her locked up in her gift.

Her stomach began to ache and she wanted to vomit.

Outside she heard the car door of a vehicle open and then shut. She hoped it was Adam and Arthur. She needed help. She sighed with relief when she heard the front door open, but it was not Adam. It was not Arthur. It was a tall woman with gnarled fingers and long, white hair held back in two low pig tails.

"Mama?" She heard Lane whimper. And he rushed to her and wrapped his arms around her tight.

"What is going on Lane? Who is this girl?" She asked him sweetly.

"Mama," he said, letting his arms drop from her waist. He didn't know how to answer her question.

"What is wrong with you, girl?" She asked.

Kate closed her mouth to try to dig up enough saliva to speak. She moved her leg to sit up a little straighter. She opened her mouth to speak but nothing came out.

"Lane?" She said, turning to him.

When he didn't answer she turned back to Kate and said, "you look very sick." The woman bent beside her and put her hand on Kate's knee as she looked closer into her face.

"I think you need a doctor. Can you tell me your name?" She asked.

Kate mouthed her name, but still she couldn't find her voice.

"Loraine!" Lane yelled out unexpectedly and Kate watched as recognition passed across his mother's face. Her eyes were open wide and she quickly took her hand from her knee.

She stepped back and looked down at Kate who was trying to shake her head.

"Lane, tell mama what happened," she said to him harshly, standing up.

Lane stopped crying and wiped his face, smearing the dirt and turning it dark.

"She just came here," he told her.

"Girl, who are you?" She yelled to Kate.

Kate squirmed trying to find her voice and eventually she was able to make an airy gasp that sounded enough like 'Kate' that she was able to figure it out.

"Kate. Did you come here to bother my son, to make fun of him?" She asked with disdain.

Kate nodded her head for no.

"Tell me what she did to you," she said to Lane as she walked to him and cradled him in her arms.

"She knows about Loraine," he said to her with fake-sounding sobs.

The woman looked down at Kate who was a mess on the floor.

"She does?" The woman said. After a few moments she added, "well, we'll have to fix that."

Through blurry eyes she watched the woman roll up her sleeves and tell Lane to get the truck and pull it up to the front door. She went to the drawers below the counters and rummaged through until she found what she was looking for. She moved toward Kate and bent down beside her. She could feel the woman's cold fingers wrap around her own wrists and pull them behind her. Kate flopped over; she could not find the strength to sit up straight anymore and fighting being tied up was not an option. As she fell over, her head hit the floor hard, making her vision blur even more. She felt a trickle of blood running down over her ear.

She tried to scream but all that came out was a harsh, whispery sound.

The imagery she had been able to see had drained her body of energy. It had drained her body of everything.

After the woman tied her hands behind her back she got to her feet and went out the screen door. Outside she could hear Lane pulling the truck up to the front porch. What was this woman going to do with her?

Kate began to think of other things, anything other than Lane, anything other than where she was at right then. She needed to fill her mind with things that made her warm so she could break out the paralysis she was in.

She closed her eyes and thought about Abby. She let all her memories flow behind her eyelids. There was the Cheerleading Competition they won in sophomore year, shopping in the mall and trying to get the attention of the boys. She remembered trying on lipstick for the first time with Abby, stealing firecrackers from her mother's purse and babysitting together so they could save money for Kate to buy rollerblades. She passed over the pain she would feel when transitioning to Adam. She didn't allow that to come, but instead she rested her mind on the thoughts of the warmth of Adam's arm, him holding onto her in bed at night, how his eyes were an embrace of their own. She breathed in deep and let it out slowly.

With her eyes still closed, she rolled her head around in circles, loosening up her muscles. She was lying on her side. Having her arms tied behind her made it nearly impossible to sit up. As she began trying, the woman came back into the house.

"Please," Kate said with a harsh voice. Her voice revealed that her throat was raw.

"What did you tell Lane about that girl?" She asked angrily. Kate didn't quite understand and even if she did, she doubted she would be able to tell her anything.

Then, to Kate's utter amazement, the woman reared her hand back and slapped her across the face. Kate's head flung to the side and her hair stuck to her cheek. She could taste blood in her mouth where her lip had busted open.

"How do you know anything?" She yelled into Kate's face.

"Lane, tell me what you told her!" She yelled to him, turning her attention from Kate.

Lane hesitated, but after a few scolds and demands, he told his mother he had told Kate what happened to Loraine.

"Do you know what you have done?" She yelled at him with her fists on her hips. "Do you know what you've caused now, you idiot?" She yelled some more. "Because you told her, now we have to kill her. Why, Lane? Why didn't you listen to me? I know what's best for you, I'm your mother!" And then she paused, looking at him in disdain.

Lane had retreated inside of himself. He sat on the kitchen floor with his fists clenched and held close to his ears. He rocked back and forth and cried softly. The woman walked over to him and kicked him in the legs calling, "get up, get up you stupid brute. Get yourself up and get cleaning up your mess and by that I mean to get rid of her."

And now he sat with hands on the floor and looked up at his mother, crying and sobbing. The woman changed her demeanor and she knelt down beside him.

"Lane, don't cry. Mama only does what is best for you. I'm only doing what will keep you safe. You don't want to go to the bad place, do you?" Lane shook his head. She cradled his head in her arms and stared at Kate, who still lay on the floor bleeding.

"Mama will make sure you don't go," she said and then she pushed him at arm's length and said to him, "but you have to do exactly what I say, OK?" Lane shook his head for yes.

"Please," Kate was able to say fully and loudly. It erupted from her like vomit.

The woman turned to her and stared at her with a hatred that was pure. "This is what you get for taking advantage of a retard boy, little girl. All you kids do nothing but make Lane's life horrible. Not a one of you know how good he is, how kind he is and that's because you just see him as a stupid kid, a retard boy, but he's more than that and you'd know it if you tried. But you never tried. And I'm not letting anyone, ANYONE, take my son away from me for any reason." She stood over Kate, making sure what she had said was sinking in with her.

"Open the tailgate, Lane," she called to him. Lane got quickly to his feet and propped open the screen door. She could hear the clunk and metal scraping metal as he let down the tailgate of the bed of the truck.

The woman grabbed a handful of Kate's hair and Kate cringed with pain. The woman pulled Kate around by her hair and drug her to the door. Kate could see the smear of blood that followed the path of her head. The blood on her lips was dry and sticky. Again she tried concentrating on good memories to rid her psyche of Lane, his mother and the accident with Loraine. She could feel the blood rising in her face and her head pounded fiercely. She felt stronger.

"Please, I know it was an accident. I'm not going to tell anyone," she pleaded. She tried to loosen the knot on her wrists, but it was no use. The knot was so tight and the string was so thin she couldn't get any leverage. She tried to break it, but the harder she pulled the tighter the rope got. It cut into her wrists and was more uncomfortable than ever.

The woman grabbed a handful of Kate's hair again and pulled her face directly into her face. The smell of the woman's breath was putrid and her teeth were rotted.

"You look here, girl. I'm not stupid like my son. I know better and I'll take no chances. Curiosity killed the cat. You should have just stayed away," she hissed and growled. She released Kate's hair roughly, throwing Kate's head back against the door jamb.

"Lane!" She called and Lane came running around the side of the truck.

The woman nodded suggesting putting Kate in the back of the truck. Lane picked Kate up by the shoulders and was pulling her near the truck bed when his mother called out, "wait!"

Lane set Kate down and his mother came back out the door with a roll of duct tape. Kate knew it was for her mouth, but the woman went straight for her feet. With every bit of strength she had been gathering Kate kicked her feet wildly, trying to break free. To her relief they flailed back and forth as her brain was commanding. One foot flew up so hard it smacked the woman in the face who quickly took a few steps back. Kate's heart was pumping and she could see that she had busted the woman's nose. The woman's blood was flowing through the fingers of the hand that covered her nose.

"You little bitch!" She cried and ran into the house. Lane ran after her. Kate began hurriedly trying to stand. She would run into the woods and hopefully very far away before they came back outside. She flopped and flopped but could not roll to the other side. She could not roll to her back. She curled in her legs to sit up on them. She was able to roll to sit on her knees but she was exhausted. She took a few breaths and tried to stand, but it was useless. Her heart was pounding so hard and all she could immerse herself in was the situation at hand. She wasn't able to find those memories that were making her stronger.

She thought about her mother and decorating the house for Christmas. She remembered when she didn't make cheerleader the first year of high school and crying in her mother's arms. And now she lifted herself up, shakily. She was standing. Now all she had to do was run. *Just run,* she thought to herself. And then out loud, "just run." She sucked in a deep breath and hoped against hope that when she lifted her legs they would run the way she instructed them. Just as she lifted her right leg to run she felt a huge whap against her thigh. The pain was searing and she instantly heard her bone break. She cried out so loudly that she was certain someone had heard her. She had hoped someone was driving by at that time or that there were neighbors down the winding road in the wooded area. She fell instantly and white flashes penetrated her vision. Spurts of white hot pain travelled through her in waves.

"Kick me again now you little twit," she heard the woman say. Kate had fallen to her side with her broken leg over top her non-broken one. The woman roughly rolled her to her back and Kate cried out more as she felt her separated bones moving. Tears sprung from her eyes as she yelled out in pain.

"Give me that damn tape," she said to Lane who was standing over them. As she yanked it from him she dropped what she had hit Kate's leg with and Kate saw it was a big hammer. The woman began to wrap Kate's ankles together and Kate screamed in pain as no regard was given to her injured leg.

"Shut up, you big baby. It ain't that bad," the woman said. And then she stopped wrapping the feet and drew out a long piece of tape. She straddled Kate and put one end of the tape right in the middle of Kate's forehead. She wrapped the tape around Kate's head, over her eyes, around her head again, over her mouth and around her head and mouth a few more times to make sure no one could hear her scream anymore. Kate was thankful that her nose was not wrapped, it was the only way she could breathe.

The woman finished wrapping the tape around Kate's ankles and halfway up her legs. The pain was excruciating. *This is it,* she said to herself. *This is how I die. I'm going to die.*

Lane lifted her by the shoulders again. Kate's cries of pain were muffled by the layers of tape as he dragged her into the truck bed. The truck rattled and shook as he shut the tailgate. Her leg was in intense pain as she lay on her side with the broken leg on top. She heard Lane get into the passenger seat and she heard his mother struggle to get into the driver's seat.

Kate looked around trying to find something sharp she could use to cut the rope on her wrists. But there was nothing in the truck bed except dirt and pebbles. Kate looked over the side of the truck as they drove. She could see nothing but trees and brush. The land rolled slightly with small hills. She wondered if she would be able to open the tailgate without the two of them in the cab hearing it. She could just slide off.

Whatever additional bones broke would be fine with her, as long as she could get away from the crazy woman. The sun had gone down. It was just after twilight, but there were no stars in the sky because of the cloud cover. Kate began to think about her mother, left alone with two missing girls. How could she let this happen?

How could she have been so stupid? She had heard Nabhanya's voice telling her not to go, but she had ignored it. She could be safe right now. She could be warm and happily too close to Adam in his truck on the way home. She could be happy and warm. But no, she hadn't listened to Nabhanya and now she was tied up and duct taped in the back of a truck with a crazy woman taking her to her imminent death. Why didn't she just listen?

The truck came to a screeching halt and Kate's body slid to the front of the truck bed. She could hear the gravel beneath them being pushed away by the instant stopping of the tires. A wave of pain from her leg shot through her. It was so bad that it blinded her for a moment; she had never felt that much pain before. They had not gone far, Kate estimated maybe five miles. For a moment nothing happened, for a moment there was silence. Then she heard Lane's door squeak and scrape open and she saw his top half over the truck making his way to the tailgate. He looked into the bed of the truck; she wondered if he was making sure she was still there. Then he quickly looked away and went back to the cab. He got in and shut the door. She heard the truck start up again and this time they were in reverse going down a hill. The movement caused Kate's body to slide down to the bottom of the bed near the tailgate. As her feet hit the tailgate her knees buckled and searing pain traveled up her spine. She screamed as loud as she possibly could but she knew she was no louder than a small bird. Her eyes filled with tears and they fell profusely. Her head was pounding very hard.

She could feel the truck rolling backward down this steep hill for about a half mile until it stopped. Lane got out of the passenger seat quickly and ran to the back of the truck. He lifted the latch on the tailgate and as it released the angle of the hill caused Kate's body to simply slide off of the truck bed and onto the ground. The pain in her leg was so severe when she hit the ground that she lost consciousness.

CHAPTER ELEVEN

When she came to she didn't know how much time had passed. She was lying face down in the cold dirt and she could hear someone dropping more dirt on top of her. She couldn't move because she was too weak. She tried to jiggle an arm but it was as if her arm muscles weren't connected to the fibers in her brain anymore. She couldn't move anything. She couldn't scream either. She was paralyzed. All she could do was lie there and listen to the dirt that was being piled on top of her. She realized she couldn't feel the pain in her leg or in her head anymore. Her vision was blurring in and out and soon she was unconscious again.

The smell of fresh laundry opened her senses to a dream-like state. There were clouds all around her in a full moon-lit night. She could hear the crickets chirping and the bullfrogs croaking. As the fog cleared from around her she stood on the edge of a sharp and rocky cliff. The smell of fresh linens faded into salty sea air and she could hear waves crashing against the jagged rocks below. In the distance, for as far as she could see, there was nothing but ocean.

The sound of a car door shutting made her turn abruptly. She saw a man leaning down into the passenger side of his vehicle.

"Excuse me!" She shouted to him. She wanted to know where she was and she thought he'd be able to tell her.

She walked quickly to him, calling to him but he paid her no attention. When she was standing beside him she tapped him on the shoulder with the thought that he might be deaf. But he still paid her no attention. She noticed his arms were thick and there was something familiar about the way he smelled. She couldn't see what he was doing in the passenger side but she heard him grunt as he picked something up. When he backed out carrying a limp body Kate looked into his face and saw that it was Lane. It was a younger, leaner Lane. The body in his arms had the same dark, side-parted hair as Kate. She had the same tone of skin. As he carried her to the cliff side the body's arm flopped to the side and Kate could see the same set of moles along her elbow that Kate had. She knew it was Loraine.

"Lane!" She called to him, even though she knew he wouldn't answer. She followed him and watched as he sat down on the ground with Loraine in his arms. He rocked her back and forth and kissed her forehead repeatedly as he cried, letting his tears fall onto her pasty white face and blue-gray lips. He held her to him tightly. And then he laid her flat on the ground and nudged her toward the edge. Her arm flopped over the side and he nudged her again. Now her shoulder was off the edge. For a third time Lane nudged Loraine's body with more force and the whole left side of her body was nearly over the edge. She could hear the frustration in Lane's voice as he stood up. He angrily lifted her body over his head and threw her into the air, out and over into the large ravine.

"Nooooo!" Kate yelled as she ran to the edge. She watched as the ocean receded to the opposite coast as Loraine's body fell. The rocks that were left behind that had been carved by the rushing water were sharp and piercing. Loraine was falling very slowly, so slowly Kate wondered if she could jump and catch up to her, to hold her while they fell, to comfort her. Tears rolled down her face.

She looked to her side to see Lane watching Loraine fall too. His face was wet with tears. There was a cracking noise and suddenly the earth began to shake. The earth trembled violently and Kate could not keep her balance so she crouched low to the ground. Lane seemed not to be affected by the tremors. He had turned and was walking slowly back to his vehicle. Now the cracking noise was louder and Kate saw the crack form in the rock bed between her and the road. And then she could feel a small piece of the cliff break away and she knew she was standing in the wrong place. She tried to get to her feet to jump to a safer part of the cliff, but the trembling raged on and she couldn't get up. The piece of cliff broke away and began to fall to the bottom of the ravine.

Kate screamed and tried to hold onto the rock but there was nothing to hold onto. She began to cry as the wind took the breath from her chest. Her breath was being taken out of her in waves, which was different. It was a strange sensation; her breath was being taken away again and again.

She began to feel like something was punching her in the chest and each time it would take her breath away.

There was one punch, two punches. For a moment there was nothing but the sensation of falling and then there was a third punch that was so powerful it took her breath away for so long she began gasping. As her eyes grew bigger the scene around her disappeared and she saw a bright light with two shadows lingering above her.

She could hear beeping and mumbling, but nothing was clear. The light was so bright it was blinding. The pain in her leg returned and it was bad, her head began to hurt again as well. She felt her lip pulsing from the wound that had been inflicted. Things were getting clearer and she could see the two shadows were people wearing hospital masks and scrubs. She deduced she was in a hospital, lying in a bed. The first few breaths were difficult, but they grew easier.

"How are you doing, Kate?" She heard a lady's voice say from beneath the hospital mask.

Kate opened her mouth but her voice was too raspy to understand. She had tried to say, 'where am I?' even though she knew.

The image of her mother came into view. Her face was tear-stained and her hair was unkempt. She felt her mother grab her hand up and hold onto it. She brushed the hair from her face and rested her other hand on Kate's cheek.

"Oh Kate, Kate," she said, burying her head into the blanket at Kate's side.

"I'm OK," Kate said to her mother. Her voice was distinguishable now.

Kate's mother lifted her head to Kate's face and tucked a piece of hair behind Kate's ear.

"What in the world made you do this? You were almost killed. You've never done anything like this in your life, going off on overnights with boys, lying to me and to your friends and thinking you could catch a kidnapper on your own. What were you thinking?" She said, crying into the sheet again.

"I'm alright, mama," she said. And her mother whimpered and put her forehead to Kate's forehead.

"You're grounded for the rest of your life," she said and Kate attempted a chuckle and, just as expected, it hurt too much so she cut it short.

Her mother lifted her head and wiped the tears from her face.

"Kate," she said with a desperate look on her face. "Please, please don't ever do anything like this again. Please understand the seriousness of it and please tell me you'll never lie to me again. Please."

Kate smiled at her mother and was about to promise her when she heard squeaky sneakers running down the hallway and coming to a screeching stop at her door. Adam came into view. He stood beside her mother.

"Kate, you're OK," he sighed. Kate was more than delighted to see his face. Her heart jumped in her chest when she was reminded that all that had happened between them was not a dream. She lifted her hand from under her mother's and put it on top of Adam's. She smiled at him to let him know she really was OK. Over Adam's head she could see Arthur's hair and eyes. His eyes were filled with concern for her. She began to feel thankful for them being in her life. But something was plaguing her.

"How did I get out?" She asked. Adam answered.

"I woke up and you were gone, I thought you were sleeping upstairs. When Arthur woke up we wanted food and that's when we discovered you had left," he began. "I tried calling your cell phone, but you had left it on the table."

"I could feel yo--" he started and then stopped as he glanced at Kate's mother. Kate knew what he was trying to tell her. He had been able to feel her and to know she was in danger.

"We got Arthur's friend's car and drove out to the Delaney's, but Arthur's car wasn't there, no one was there. We drove around for an hour, thinking maybe you'd gone out for food but we never saw Arthur's car. We went back to Celia's to see if you'd come back but nothing. We waited for another hour to see if you'd show up and you didn't so we called the police and your mother," he explained.

"If it wasn't for Adam no one would have even went to look for you out there," her mother said.

Adam smiled and his face blushed.

"He was quite the attack dog," Arthur chimed in.

"They said they had to wait for 24 hours to see if you'd come back, but, well, I guess I'm persuasive. They started searching the area and found you in the woods by a creek. They said you were covered in dirt and branches and leaves."

"You were very lucky," her mother said to her. "You had been there bleeding and broken for," she said before she had to stop and take in a deep breath to maintain her composure. "For ten hours." The composure couldn't be contained and another round of tears spilled over the rims of her eyes. They came in torrents. She could see Arthur's arm make its way around her mother's shoulder to comfort her, which made Kate very appreciative of him. She saw her mother's hand reach up to pat Arthur's in thanks and somehow she knew this family was going to work, even before it had the chance to begin. Or had it?

"What happened to Lane?" She asked.

Kate's mother wiped her tears and a stone cold look came over her face. She watched her mother transform into something angry she'd never seen before.

"He'll be in prison for a long time," she said through clenched teeth.

"No," Kate said. "No, he didn't mean it. It was an accident. He…he didn't understand, Mom."

Her mother looked at her bewildered.

"Kate," she said heavily. "How can you take up for the man who killed your sister, the man that almost killed *you*?"

It was becoming apparent to Kate that the police must have been able to get the story from either Lane or his mother. They would have told Kate's mother about it as well. She didn't like it at all, she had wanted to be the one to tell her mother what had happened to Loraine.

"He didn't…it wasn't like that. He loved her, mama. He--" she tried to explain.

"Loved her? Loved her?" Kate's mother was almost yelling. She stood up straight.

"Kate, he put heroin into her body and killed her by overdosing her," she said. Her voice rose and she was yelling.

"He threw her body over a cliff! He broke your leg and buried you alive! These are not accidents!"

Arthur tightened her grip around her mother's shoulder to relax her as he whispered, "shhh, whoa now."

"No, he didn't know what it was he was giving her. There were boys that were mean to him and tricked him into doing it. They told him that it'd make her very happy. He didn't understand. He didn't know it would kill her. When he realized she wasn't going to wake up anymore he was scared, he was so scared, mama, and he was hurting. He was hurting so bad because he had killed the one person in his life who wanted anything to do with him, the one person who never made fun of him or tried to hurt him. It was his mother who broke my leg," Kate's mother was listening intently.

"It was his mother who decided to try to kill me, not Lane. Lane told me everything about Loraine, mom. He told me the whole story and he cried and was hurting so bad." Tears welled in Kate's eyes as she remembered how heavy Lane's despair had played on her, how deep that pain must have went to drain Kate's energy completely from her as she felt what he was feeling."

"His mother?" Adam asked.

"Yeah, she's crazy, Adam. She's nuts. When she found out that Lane had told me what had happened to Loraine, she demanded that he kill me. When I fought back she broke my leg with a hammer. She's the one who tied me up and duct taped my legs together and my mouth and eyes shut. It was her," she explained.

Before Kate was even finished telling the story Arthur had dialed the police on his phone. He walked out of her view, but she could hear him asking for someone. She couldn't hear the name of the person, but she could hear Arthur telling the person what she had just told him.

She looked at her mother and could see all the pain of losing Loraine passing through her mother's eyes. She tried not to let her mother's feelings latch onto her, but she wasn't able to fight and the pain and sadness of deep loss washed over her body in crashing waves. The pain of the ultimate loss ripped through her heart and she felt all her mother was feeling.

"Mom you got to stop," she said as she felt herself getting weaker. Something had awakened inside of her, some ability to retain the feelings of the people around her. Images flashed through her mind of her mother in the throes of child birth and the pain between Kate's own legs seared. She saw a baby being placed in her mother's arms and heard her mother whisper, "Loraine." She felt all the joy and the happiness that her mother was feeling, but as soon as it flashed behind her eyes it dissipated and converted into a crying baby in the middle of the night. Frustration and exhaustion filled her.

Even though these things were passing through her she could hear the reactions of the others.

"Kate, what's wrong?" her mother pressed. And then "get the doctor" and her mother became frantic, which doubled inside of Kate. She couldn't turn it off, it wouldn't stop. Her heart raced as her mother's whole life with Loraine passed through her mind and the emotions filled her so much she couldn't escape it. Then, as soon as it came, it went. Everything was fine. Kate could only feel her own emotions and though she searched for her mother's memory, she saw it no more.

"I'm fine," she said, grasping her mother's hand. Arthur, who had started out the door to get a nurse, turned to look to make sure she was OK. She must have appeared to be fine because he came back into the room.

"What was that?" Adam asked. She wondered how come he didn't know. She imagined he'd never be able to 'guess' what was happening to her. As much as she loved her mother and enjoyed Arthur she wanted them to leave. She wanted to talk to Adam alone. She wanted to tell him the whole story. She wanted to tell him she knew everything she knew because she could see it happening and she could feel the feelings people were feeling, or had felt in the past.

As they settled back down there was silence among them. Her mother held her hand and stared at her mostly. Adam stood beside her and Arthur sat in a chair by the door.

"When can I go home?" She asked when a nurse came in to check her equipment.

"I'm not sure just yet, but we'll know when the doctor sees you again at two," she answered without looking at Kate. She seemed friendly enough, but also distracted.

"Boy you're going to be pretty popular when you get home. You're going to have quite a story to tell," her mother said. And then jumping in her seat startled with a sudden realization she said, "Oh honey, I didn't even think to call Abby." Her mother turned and grabbed up her purse to look for her cell phone.

"I already did," Adam said, looking away.

Kate looked at him confused.

"You did? When? Did she say she was coming?" Kate's mother asked.

Adam only shook his head. Kate could tell he had told Abby what had happened between them. He had to have told her.

"You told her?" Kate asked. Kate's mother looked from Kate to Adam and then back to Kate.

"Told who what?" She asked.

Kate sighed loudly and rubbed her head.

"I didn't know what else to do," Adam said, shrugging. "I had to tell her you were hurt, I had to tell her. How else could I explain why you were with me?"

"I know," Kate said, sighing again. She knew it was best to have told her when he did; she imagined it must have been hell for him to hold that secret from her. She hadn't thought about it before now, but she imagined it must have been killing him inside to be hurting Abby, just as it was killing her inside to be hurting Abby.

"She didn't come?" Kate asked.

"Tell her what?" Kate's mother asked loudly.

Kate looked at her mother, not knowing where to begin. To her relief Arthur chimed in.

"Abby and Adam were a pair and now Kate and Adam are a pair," he said, making it simple.

"Ooooh," her mother said. "So you're seeing an ex-boyfriend of Abby's. Well, I'm sure she'll be fine, give her a call."

"No," Adam said. It wasn't the whole story.

"Adam is Abby's current boyfriend. Well, probably not after she told him about this weekend," Kate told her mother.

"Wait. What?" She said.

Kate didn't know how to tell her mother that she had started seeing Abby's boyfriend while he was still Abby's boyfriend.

"What do you mean, after this weekend?" Her mother asked with suspicion in her voice. Kate smiled because she knew her mother must have been thinking she had sex with Adam. It was embarrassing to have to talk about that with her mother in front of Adam and Arthur.

"Well, put simply, Kate took Abby's boyfriend," Arthur said.

"It wasn't like that," Kate and Adam said at the same time.

"Then what was it like?" Her mother asked, still wondering if her daughter had done the deed.

"It's a long story," she told her. "And no, there was no sex," she added to reassure her mother.

She saw her mother's shoulders relax and after a few moments she said, "Boy I feel like I don't know my own daughter at all."

"Well, I didn't know exactly how to tell anyone. I was just confused and--" she started, but couldn't finish. She wanted to cry. It was all too much for her. And then it hit her: "the thing lost will be forever." Her heart pitted in her stomach and she knew. She knew the friendship she'd had all those years was gone now. It was going to be something Abby would not be able to forgive. Perhaps time would change her mind, but Kate guessed it would be long after they had left high school and parted ways. She could remember Nabhanya's vision of Abby traveling the world and learning to become a chef or a baker. She knew what would happen. Abby was lost to her forever. The tears came, steady and silently they slid down her cheeks. She looked around the room at all she had left in the world. She had lost Abby but she had Adam, her mother and Arthur. She remembered Nabhanya's words "but you will gain something else."

Printed in Great Britain
by Amazon.co.uk, Ltd.,
Marston Gate.